Dear Reader,

Ho...
the...
tha...
pro... ld
a re...

An... offer you the Harlequin Heartwarming series. Each of these special stories is a wholesome, heartfelt romance imbued with the traditional values so important to you. They are books you can share proudly with friends and family. And the authors featured in this collection are some of the most talented storytellers writing today, including favorites such as Janice Kay Johnson, Margaret Daley and Shelley Galloway. We've selected these stories especially for you based on their overriding qualities of emotion and tenderness, and they center around your favorite themes—children, weddings, second chances, the reunion of families, the quest to find a true home and, of course, sweet romance.

So curl up in your favorite chair, relax and prepare for a heartwarming reading experience!

Sincerely,

The Editors

CYNTHIA REESE

lives with her husband and their daughter in south
Georgia, along with their two dogs, three cats and
however many strays show up for morning muster.
She has been scribbling since she was knee-high
to a grasshopper and reading even before that.
A former journalist, teacher and college English
instructor, she also enjoys cooking, traveling and
photography when she gets the chance.

HARLEQUIN HEARTWARMING

Cynthia Reese

A Place to Call Home

HARLEQUIN®
entertain, enrich, inspire™

Recycling programs
for this product may
not exist in your area.

ISBN-13: 978-0-373-36610-1

A PLACE TO CALL HOME

Copyright © 2013 by Cynthia R. Reese

Originally published as NOT ON HER OWN
Copyright © 2008 by Cynthia R. Reese

Printed in U.S.A.

A Place to Call Home

To two very special women:

In memory of my mom, whom I miss every day,
and dedicated as well to Laura Shin,
for making my dreams come true.

This book would not be a reality without the
intensive help I received from my wonderful
editor, Victoria Curran. She literally saved this
project. I'd also like to thank Marsha Zinberg,
Laura Barth, and all the folks at Heartwarming.
Thanks, too, to my sister, Donna, for helping
me through the early planning stages, and my
critique partners, Tawna Fenske, Cindy Miles,
Stephanie Bose and Nelsa Roberto; to my dad,
who helped answer some of the technical aspects
of welding; and to Tawna and her friends
Larie and Minta for helping me with how
Oregonians plan weddings—all errors are mine!

CHAPTER ONE

NO GOOD DEED ever goes unpunished, and Brandon Wilkes, who'd sworn to serve and protect the good people of Brazelton County, Georgia, was living proof of that.

"You sure? Brandon, are you positively sure?"

Brandon clamped his jaw shut, trying not, in his effort to get to work on time, to lose his patience with Prentice O'Keefe. The man had the comprehension of an eight-year-old, and the comic-book-violence imagination to go with it.

"Prentice, I swear. No aliens are going to come down here and get you and take you back to their planet. It was just a movie. Okay? Just make-believe."

"But they could, couldn't they? I mean, they were big, Brandon and…" Here Prentice's lower lip trembled. "Scary. Bad scary."

Prentice's older sister, Ella, pushed open

the raggedy screen door. "Prentice, he's told you that there's no such thing as aliens! Now why can't you believe him? Man's got to get to work and he's come all this way out of town to tell you not to believe such garbage!"

"It's okay, Ella," Brandon said, suppressing an urge to look at his watch. His boss might not agree that reassuring Prentice justified Brandon's being late, but Brandon knew, for Ella's sake, it was important. "Coming by here was on my way to see my uncle—and I've got time before I have to clock in at the sheriff's department. Besides, I don't want Prentice worrying about things. I know how he gets his mind fixed."

"Tell me about it. Those so-called friends of his—filling his head with such nonsense and letting him watch crazy movies. He'll be going on about this for days." Ella threw up her hands, pulled open the screen door that barely hung on its hinges, and went inside. "I give up."

Prentice poked out his bottom lip even more. "I ain't stupid. I know things. Y'all don't tell me things, but I can figure it out."

Brandon's impatience melted away. Prentice was his age, thirty, and Brandon had seen others tease him all through school. The least he could do was not belittle Prentice's fears.

"Here, I've got something in the car that will fix you right up, Prentice." Brandon jogged to the cruiser, yanked open the glove compartment and dug out a toy plastic star from a packet of dozens of identical plastic stars he kept for kids. Then he crossed the weedy front yard back to the O'Keefes' porch.

"Okay, Prentice, you know what this is, right?"

Prentice's eyes rounded. "Ooh, boy, Brandon! That's a badge! Like yours!" He reached out to touch it, then snatched his hand back.

"No, no, it's yours. But wait. We've got to make this official. Hold up your right hand." Brandon led Prentice through a halting oath of office, using a lot of invention when his memory failed him. "Okay, then. If any aliens come around in their flying saucers, you tell 'em you're a sure enough Brazelton County deputy, and they'd better leave you alone."

"Ha! I will, Brandon! Yes, sir! Hey, Ella!

Brandon made me a deputy! And he says there is, too, aliens, and they won't mess with me—"

Brandon shook his head as Prentice disappeared into the house.

He didn't linger, though. He was late for work already, and his planned trip by Uncle Jake's would have to be put off—he'd never dreamed Ella's request would take up so much time.

A WOMAN STOOD in the middle of the highway.

Brandon groaned. This day was already shaping up to be a beaut. What was it? A full moon or something? He pulled the sheriff's cruiser to a stop, rolled down the window and poked his head out.

"Ma'am?"

The woman didn't seem to notice. Not him. Not the fact that the bumper of his Crown Vic was less than three feet from her. Certainly not that she was standing at the base of a hill, on a curve, square in the middle of the double-yellow line.

"Ma'am!"

This time she turned, her dark ringlets sliding back over shoulders bare except for the thin straps of her sundress. She was a little thing, no bigger than five-two, and that was with help from the high-heeled sandals she wore.

Brandon tore his gaze from her tanned legs—surprisingly long for a gal as short as she was—and her toned arms and looked back up at the woman's face.

And then at her hand.

She held up one index finger, the classic sign for wait. Then she turned her attention back to the hill in front of her.

Brandon scratched his head and considered the problem. The lady was pretty, sure, but what kind of woman dressed up in her Sunday best and stood in the middle of a highway? What was she up to?

And she was telling a sheriff's deputy to wait?

He pulled the cruiser over to the edge of the road and prepared to cue the radio on his shoulder. Better to let the dispatcher know he was dealing with a possible fruit-loop, as if he hadn't already had his fruit-loop quotient filled to the brim with Prentice's aliens.

But before he could speak into the shoulder pack, it crackled. He released the button and waited.

"Brandon, you in the car yet?"

"Yeah. I've got a—"

"Listen, how close are you to county road one twenty-one?"

"I'm on it, matter of fact."

"Out close to your uncle's?"

"Near there. Wade, listen, I've got a woman—"

"We're going to need you to provide an escort."

"A what?"

Just then he heard a rumble on the highway—the rumble of an oncoming eighteen-wheeler.

"Wade, pedestrian in the road, gotta go!"

Brandon shoved open his door. Sure enough, he could hear the gears shifting as the truck gathered speed.

"Ma'am! There's a truck coming! You need to get off the road!"

She waved one hand in his direction, brushing him away. With her other hand, she lifted a small digital camera to her eye.

Blowing out a breath, Brandon crossed the

hot tarry asphalt to her. "Ma'am, I've asked you nicely—" He went behind her, to lift her up at the waist and remove her bodily from the path of the oncoming vehicle.

"Put me down! What on earth—" The tanned legs windmilled on him, and one high-heeled shoe caught him square on the shin.

"Ow! Lady, are you crazy?"

"Put me down! I'm going to miss it!" She jerked from his grasp in a lightning-quick move that nearly threw him on the roadway—some sort of tai chi or martial arts move. He recovered his balance and took a step backward.

The truck crested the hill, bearing down on them. Brandon looked up to see the cab of the truck dwarfed by a...

"A house?"

He blinked. Yes. It was a house. Somebody was moving a house down the middle of the narrow county road. Could this day get any more surreal?

The woman took her time snapping photos of the truck snailing along at maybe thirty miles an hour, if that, with its road-wide load.

Photos apparently done, she strolled to the road's shoulder to stand by Brandon's cruiser. He followed her. As he tried to frame an apology, his radio crackled again.

"Uh, Brandon?"

"I think I figured it out, Wade. The escort's for a house?"

"Yeah. Just make sure they don't tear any power lines down, okay?"

Brandon spotted a man sitting astride the roof of the house, a long plastic pole in his hands. He blinked again, but the man was still there.

It was weird to see a house on the back of a truck cruising down a narrow highway. Sure, he'd seen plenty of double-wides delivered, but never an actual house.

And this was indeed a house. He examined it as it trundled past and the man on the roof used the pole to lift up a power line.

The house looked big because of the scale of the road, but Brandon could see that it was no more than a cottage. It had been yellow at one time; now it was in dire need of a new coat or three of paint. Looked like an arts and crafts type cottage, maybe built in the late thirties or forties. Not a window in the thing was intact, and the porch roof was held up by boards fastened to the side of the house.

He glanced from the house to the woman who now, he'd figured out too late, must belong with it.

"Uh…sorry about that. I thought—"

She turned to him, beaming. "That's my house! My very first house!"

"Well. Congratulations. But next time I'd advise not standing in the middle of the road to get a picture of it."

Brandon rubbed his cheek and considered. No way was he going to be able to get in front of the truck now, so his escort services would wind up being follow-me services.

"Where's it headed?" he asked her.

"My land. Oh, I'm sorry, I'm Penelope Langston." She extended a small hand bare of rings and fingernail polish.

Brandon accepted the handshake. "Deputy Brandon Wilkes. So you're—"

And then it hit him. Her name.

"Did you say Langston?"

"Yes. Penelope Langston. That was very sweet, what you did for me a moment ago—"

"As in Langston Holdings?"

He couldn't keep the edge out of his tone.

"Yes. That's my company."

A bitter taste coated the inside of Brandon's mouth, a wash of nausea flooding him. Langston Holdings. The mysterious holding company that had bid up his uncle's land when it went to auction—again—and Brandon had been unable to save his uncle's farm. Again.

Uncle Jake tried to keep a stiff upper lip about losing half the acreage he'd farmed all his life, but Brandon knew the way he'd lost it had been the real kicker. Richard Murphy, a big-time area farmer, had colluded with the county tax commissioner to dummy up tax debts.

That's what had happened to Uncle Jake and Brandon. Brandon had been a full partner in his uncle's small farming operation when the tax commissioner sent them a bill they couldn't prove they'd paid. The tax commissioner had handpicked farmers like Uncle Jake, who, in years past, before computers, had tended to pay tax bills in cash and in installments. A few of the farmers had been able to produce ancient, yellowed receipts. Uncle Jake and at least one other farmer hadn't been such good record keepers. And Murphy had offered to stave off a sheriff's sale by buying part of the farm at a rock-bottom price.

Then—and here Brandon couldn't conceal a satisfied grin—Murphy himself had fallen on hard times. He was facing a federal indictment on charges a mile long on government crop insurance fraud. The corrupt farmer had seen his own land, including the acres he'd swindled out of Uncle Jake, sold by auction.

Brandon had tried to buy his uncle's property back, but a holding company out of Oregon had outbid him at the auction. Langston Holdings.

This was the enemy? This woman? She was what, late twenties? And she could go around snatching up tracts of prime farmland?

If Penelope Langston saw his reaction, she didn't act like it registered. Nope, she was as bubbly as a kid at her birthday party, ready to unwrap presents. A dimple jumped in her cheek as she grinned.

"So, where's your car?" he growled.

"Oh, back there." Penelope gestured with a thumb in the direction the house was moving. "I guess I didn't think things through, but I did want to get a picture of it. Wasn't it awesome, coming down that hill? Can you give me a lift? You are here to direct traffic, right?"

He didn't bother to suppress a snort. Traffic? Here? In South Georgia? The only traffic jams he knew of were when people had to slow down behind an old-timer like Uncle Jake or a creeping tractor.

"You're obviously not from around here. This road isn't traveled that much." He glanced from Penelope's animated face to the house and blew out a breath. "C'mon. I'll give you a ride."

"Great!"

He would have figured her for a chatterbox, but in the cruiser, she proved him wrong. Maybe it was because she was absorbed in her big day.

Brandon felt the tiniest bit churlish for thinking ill of her. So she'd beat him out of the land. It had been an auction fair and square. And at least she was putting a house on it. It wasn't as though she was turning it into a subdivision.

He turned off on a dirt road and negotiated the Crown Vic over the washboard surface.

"I thought…" Penelope frowned.

"I'm taking a shortcut. This comes out near my uncle's—your land." The correction ate at him. He forced himself to be civil and polite. "What brings you here?"

"Well, the land, of course. I'd found the house, oh, ages ago, on the internet, believe it or not. It came from North Georgia, and the owners were selling it cheap to anyone who would move it. But I needed a square of dirt to put it on."

Square of dirt? Thirty acres of the best cropland on this side of the county was more than a "square of dirt."

"And you're originally from…?"

"Portland, Oregon. You know, I can't get over how *flat* everything is here. No peaks. No mountains. No real hills, even. But the pine trees look like home."

"Oregon, huh? What, you hear about the land on the internet or something?" Brandon's curiosity got the better of him. He'd tried, without success, to dig up information on Langston Holdings and the people behind it.

Never in a million years would he have thought the people behind it would be just this slip of a woman.

"Oh, no. Family." She didn't offer more in the way of explanation, instead pointing. "Look! They're turning in! Wow! Oh, I want to get another picture!"

He turned back onto the paved road and parked on the shoulder. "Well, uh, where are they putting the house? They're not putting it there, are they? They're putting it farther back, right?"

She paused in the act of opening the car door. "Yeah. That's the prettiest spot on the whole thirty acres. Why? Do you know something I don't? It's not wetlands. I checked it out. And, see, there's a rise, but it's not high on a hill."

"That's the best part of the tract, the most fertile. We didn't even have to put half the fertilizer on that section that we did on the rest."

"You worked for Grandpa Murphy?"

His head snapped around from his view through the windshield. "*Grandpa?* You mean Richard Murphy? You're related to Richard Murphy?"

"Of course. That's how I knew about the land. He's my mother's dad." Penelope hopped out of the car. She ducked her head back in. "And anyway, as far as the land's fertility goes, it doesn't really matter. I mean, can you see *me* farming?"

Her laugh bubbled up, rich and throaty. The double whammy of the day left him numb to it.

It was bad enough Penelope was indifferent about putting something as permanent as a house on the best farming land in the area.

But to find out she was the granddaughter of the guy who'd forced Uncle Jake off his land?

She slammed the door and crossed the pastureland. The breeze caught the skirt of her sundress and with each step the heels of her shoes dug into the earth.

Two years ago, Brandon had planted soybeans here, soybeans that had produced double what the rest of his uncle's farm had produced. Now, he saw a pine seedling or two popping up out of the ground. Another two years lying fallow, and this land would be a piney thicket.

Suddenly the confines of the patrol car closed in on him. He had a good job, sure. He liked being a deputy, helping people.

So what if it wasn't farming? So what if most days he spent writing out speeding tickets along the interstate and the only time he felt the wind in his face and the sun on his back was when he was changing some traveler's flat tire? So what if the only thing he grew these days was the odd tomato plant on the excuse of a back deck he had at his apartment? He was hardly there, anyway. He spent so much of his time off at Uncle Jake's. Probably he should give up the cramped little place altogether.

Being a deputy paid the bills, right? It took care of Uncle Jake, who didn't have two cents to rub together these days.

Face it. This farming gig was just a pipe dream. You're thirty. It's time to grow up, put away childish things.

Brandon blew out a sigh and heaved himself from the cruiser to cross the field he'd once plowed.

Penelope stopped short of where the transfer truck was backing across the roughed-in driveway the county had put in. She stretched out her arms and spun around. "My dream! Dirt and a house! I've finally got dirt and a house!"

CHAPTER TWO

PENELOPE GRITTED her teeth and stretched to reach a huge glob of glazier's putty from the window. The distance between the top of the ladder and the far edge of the pane seemed insurmountable.

If she were normal height, with normal legs and normal arms, this job would be a piece of cake.

Aaargh. What I wouldn't do for a couple of inches right about now.

Penelope set her jaw. She would not quit.

Just think: do this, and you're done with the windows. Two weeks here, and you've got the house livable. Before you know it, you'll get your studio up and you can start on your project. Just think. In two months, she'd have fifty grand, and she could hire someone to finish up the house. She could do this. She could prove them all wrong, Mom,

Dad, everybody who said this was nothing but a fantasy.

Her pep talk gave her that last, vital half-inch of stretch.

"Hey! You're gonna fall!"

Startled, Penelope screeched and nearly did fall. The tube of putty careened off the ladder, along with the caulking gun. Her putty knife fell to the ground, where a million blades of grass and a couple clods of red Georgia clay stuck to the sticky white putty she'd just saved.

Penelope spotted the cause of the upset: the grouchy deputy, this time sans uniform. He wore jeans, paired with a cotton tee that showed off his chest in a way that his browns hadn't. And now that he was without the Smoky Bear hat, she could see that his dark brown hair was clipped short.

"Didn't mean to scare you. Brandon Wilkes. I was the deputy who—"

"Yes, I remember you. Sorry. I don't usually startle that easily, but I didn't hear you."

"You were busy applying that putty. Need a hand?"

"I think I've got it. It's high back here."

Brandon put his hands on his narrow hips and surveyed the bungalow. "You've had a lot done to the place in the past week or so."

"I've done most of it myself. Except, of course, for the foundation and the roof. The movers put a pier foundation under the house, and I hired a roofer."

Penelope climbed down from the ladder and joined him. She inspected the house, ticking off the progress she'd made. A new foundation, a new roof to replace the old one messed up by the move, electricity and well pump hookup, new locks.

The house was still in sore need of a paint job, but the pressure washing had improved the looks of the house immensely. A thousand more jobs awaited her.

"I—my uncle lives next door, just up the road. I figured I'd check up on you." Brandon grimaced. "I mean, check *in* on you. To see if you needed any help."

Penelope decided his slip was Freudian. Since when did grouches with badges offer assistance? She started to say something snarky about being perfectly capable of looking after herself. She stopped short, though.

Maybe she should give him the benefit of the doubt. This was the South, she reminded herself. After bouncing around big, impersonal cities like L.A. and New York, that would take her some time to get accustomed to.

"Thank you."

"I would have called…but I couldn't find a listing for you."

"I haven't bothered with a landline yet. I have a cell phone."

"You really need a landline. Our E-911 system doesn't pick up the location of cell phones. A woman like yourself, living alone out here…" Brandon trailed off. His attention dropped to her bare left hand. "I mean, I guess you're living alone out here."

Was the deputy trying to hit on her? She suppressed a smile. "It's just me and Theo."

"Theo?"

"My cat." She pointed to the window. "The Siamese?"

Brandon's gaze followed her gesture toward the long and lanky white cat peering out the windowpane.

"That's a Siamese?" he asked. "I thought they were brown."

"Flame-point. They're white, with apricot ears and paws and tail. Everything you've heard about Siamese? Well, multiply that by ten and you've got your typical flame-point."

One of Brandon's eyebrows arched. "He doesn't seem to think too much of me."

"It's me he's mad at. I've had to keep him cooped up until I could get the windows fixed. Now he's got the run of the house and he's plotting his escape back to New York."

"New York? I thought you said you were from Oregon?" Brandon treated her to intense cop-like scrutiny. What was this, an interrogation? Did he think she was lying?

"I grew up in Portland, moved to Bend when I was a teenager. But New York was my latest stop." She retrieved the putty knife and scraped the blade against the ladder. "Here." She handed it to him. "Since you're here and you offered, I'll take you up on it. Can you do me a favor and clean the rest of that putty along the top edge?"

Brandon hesitated before agreeing and clambering up the ladder. The move let Penelope see that his jeans fitted nicely over his long legs. The faded denim was as much an improvement over his browns as the T-shirt. "I'm kind of surprised you got the house set down on a foundation so quick," he observed as he deftly wielded the putty knife.

Hmm...skills and looks. Not a bad combo, not bad at all, she thought.

"It was part of the bargain with the movers. They're the ones who put me in touch with a roofer. Once you move a house, the roof has to be replaced as soon as possible, and this one especially. The whole interior has hardwood floors. I didn't want them damaged."

Back down on the ground, Brandon inspected his work and was apparently satisfied. "So the house was what? Built in the thirties? Forties?"

"Mid-thirties, despite the Depression. Want to take a look inside?" For a moment, Penelope couldn't believe she'd offered. He was a complete stranger. And a big one at that.

But her gut told her this guy was okay. Open, honest face. Nice brown eyes. A lot of smile lines.

"Sure," he told her.

Inside, Penelope pushed away doubts, say, thoughts of how harmless Ted Bundy had looked to his victims, as she showed Brandon through the house.

They ended in the dinky kitchen with its 1960s atrocity of a kitchen-remodel. Brandon stared, his uncertainty about what to say plain on his face.

"It'll get better. I'll rip out the cabinets, restore a lot of the old look," she rushed to assure him.

"It's...the whole house is...rough," he said finally.

"Yeah. But it's got great bones."

"And you're planning on doing this yourself? You must be handy with a hammer."

Brandon Wilkes scored more points with Penelope because his expression was one of admiration; not a drop of disbelief or condescension tempered it.

"I know my way around a toolbox. It's the big stuff that's hard for me. I know how to do it, but when you're a shrimp like me..."

He didn't even offer a short joke. Another point.

"Well, I'll be glad to offer some free labor if you need it. Let me know. If I can't, I'll point you in the right direction."

"Great! Maybe you could suggest someone who could help put up a barn or a shelter?"

He frowned. "Like a pole barn?"

"Pole barn?"

"Yeah, just a barn with poles for framing and then the exterior sheathing is fastened to them. Usually has a metal roof."

"Sounds about right. How tall can they be?"

"How tall do you need it?"

"Um…" She did some mental calculations. "Twenty feet at least, plus any extra I could get from the pitch of the roof."

"Whoa. What are you putting in there?"

"My work. I'm an artist. A sculptor. I do outside sculptures for businesses and corporations."

"You mean, like statues and stuff?"

"Uh…not exactly." Penelope opened the flap of a cardboard box still waiting to be unpacked on one of the dingy Formica countertops. She pulled out a small model of her latest project. "Like this."

Brandon stared at it, the same befuddled expression on his face that he'd had when he'd tried to think of something to say about the kitchen. After a long moment, he blurted, "What is it?"

Penelope slid a finger along the narrow ribbons of stainless steel. "I call it *Love at Infinity*. See the infinity symbol here? And how it wraps around these two vertical pieces?"

Brandon pointed to the highly polished surface. "There? Yeah, I see the infinity symbol. And the wavy vertical lines are supposed to be, what?" He screwed up his face as he examined the piece.

Penelope laughed at his underwhelmed expression. "You're not a fan of abstract art, are you? Those two pieces represent man and woman."

"Doesn't look much like a man or a woman to me, but…" Brandon shrugged. "I don't know much about art. So you'll build this bigger?"

"Much bigger. This tall section here tops out at just under twenty feet."

"And people actually buy things like this?"

Penelope chose to let his comment slide. What had she expected anyway? He was a completely different breed from the usual artsy crowd she ran with. "Yes, yes, they do.

Matter of fact, the commission for this one will bring me fifty thousand dollars."

Brandon whistled. "That's a lot of money for three pieces of stainless steel."

"Not just any three pieces of stainless steel. You have to know how to build it."

"And have somewhere *to* build it. I don't think a pole barn would work. Not tall enough. But I'll be thinking. Where do you plan to put the barn?"

"Out behind the house. Maybe with big sliding doors on casters or wheels. It won't look right with the house, but…" Penelope shrugged and set the sculpture down. "My work's what pays for the house, and I've got to have a studio. So I guess I can't complain."

"You know, this kind of house looks out of place in the middle of a field."

The comment took her by surprise, for one, that he would understand the aesthetics of a bungalow and its setting. For another, the sudden change in topic. "Well, yes, I guess so," Penelope said. "But I couldn't afford to be picky. Besides, I'll plant some fast-growing trees, and in a few years, it won't look the same."

She could have sworn he winced. What was so bad about trees?

"You know…I was planning—" Brandon started, then broke off.

Penelope waited him out. He started again. "At one point, this land belonged to my uncle. Well, to me and my uncle. Did you know that?"

"No. No, I wasn't aware of that." She folded her arms and waited some more. Alarm bells sounded in her head.

"Yeah. Murphy—your grandfather—I don't know how to put this politely. But he and his brother-in-law hatched up a tax scheme to put a squeeze on Uncle Jake, and my uncle was forced to sell this section of his land."

"Really." Didn't sound a bit like the story Grandpa had told her. Penelope's thoughts raced as she tried to predict where Brandon was going with this conversation.

"Yeah. Really." A sharp edge bit at Brandon's words. "This land—where you've got your house sitting—it's the best cropland of the whole tract…of Uncle Jake's old tract, I mean."

"Uh-huh." What was this guy's agenda?

Maybe her gut had steered her wrong after all.

Brandon rubbed his hands together, shuffled his feet on the scratched finish of the hardwood floor.

"I was...I came here today to see if you'd be up to making a trade. This plot of land for another. The one I had in mind is a much better site for the house. It's got maples and sweetgums, lots of shade for the summer."

"But I've already got the—"

"And we could, um, throw in the cost of moving the house...and maybe, the foundation. The cost of moving it shouldn't be that much."

She'd been wrong. This guy *was* a nut, albeit a cute one. He actually thought—

"You think I'm crazy, don't you?" he asked.

"Well, yeah. I'm inclined to that way of thinking...or that maybe there's some sort of treasure buried here."

His face heated up. "Nope. No treasure. This—it's only that I'm more than a little attached to this land. Maybe it's just that it *is* such good land. Or maybe it's because of the way my uncle lost it. I don't know."

"I'm really sorry. I can't imagine how you must feel…but I'm really happy with my land. And I don't even want to think about moving this house again. I've got two months to get my sculpture built and delivered."

Brandon looked as though he might argue. Then his jaw tightened and he stuffed his hands in his back pockets. He stood there for a long moment before moving stiffly toward the door leading to the hall.

"Well. Guess it was worth a shot. Though why I ever thought any granddaughter of Murphy would understand where I was coming from…"

She heard his footsteps echo off the empty rooms, and then the front door shut with a loud thud.

CHAPTER THREE

"TOLD YOU that girl was moving fast. Here, have some more rice and peas."

Before Brandon could stop Uncle Jake, the man had dumped a clump of sticky rice and some field peas onto Brandon's chipped stoneware plate. A cook Uncle Jake most definitely wasn't, not that he could afford better food.

"Yeah, well, I've been busy these past couple of weeks, Uncle Jake. Not only have I been working my regular nightshift, but we're short during the day, too." Brandon tried but failed to keep the defensive note out of his voice. If only he'd come up with the land swap idea sooner, before she'd reroofed the place, maybe then she'd have been more receptive.

"I know. You're always busy. That sheriff of ours keeps you bustin' your chops. Hardly ever see you these days."

Uncle Jake flopped back in his chair. After a moment of silent concentration, he attacked his own second helping of rice with gusto.

Brandon knew that look. He'd seen it often enough since he and his mom had moved in when Brandon was a skinny ten-year-old and his brother was an even skinnier eight-year-old.

"You're thinking I was wasting my time, aren't you?"

The old man looked up from his dinner plate. "Well…folks don't want to split up their land, especially not a woman who's got a house set down."

Brandon snorted. "Not much of a house if you ask me." But then, with eyes that would see it like a stranger would, he saw his uncle's dining room, with its stacks of books and newspapers, its yellowed white walls and the vinyl rug curling up in one corner. Uncle Jake took up more time repairing his pigpens than he did his own place. Since Brandon's mom had passed away three years ago, Uncle Jake had sure let the place go. The house wasn't much of an improvement over Penelope Langston's bungalow.

"I won't lie, son. It's that 'no-never' that gets you every time, the idea that I won't ever see a plow of mine on that land now." Uncle Jake paused in his eating, his rheumy old eyes far away. "I still remember the day I signed the papers to buy that land where she's put her house. I knew it was good for growing, and I couldn't wait. I didn't even have a tractor of my own yet, 'cause I'd spent every penny I'd saved just for the down payment. So I borrowed my daddy's old Massey Ferguson and broke ground that same day."

Brandon had heard the story a hundred times at least, but he didn't interrupt. A man had a right to grieve, after all. When his uncle finished, the two of them sat in silence.

"An artist, you say?" Uncle Jake asked suddenly.

"Yeah. Big metal abstract pieces. She wants to put up a barn to work in."

"You and the FFA kids gonna help her?"

He did a double take at his uncle. "Why should I help her put more things on that land that I'll have to tear down when I finally get it?"

"Son, it is obvious you don't know much

about women." Uncle Jake took a swig of his iced tea and scarfed up the last of the peas.

"Oh, and you, the lifelong bachelor, are an expert?"

His uncle grinned and waggled his eyebrows. "Why you think I never married?" But then he sobered. "See, with a man, you could have offered to swap my field, I mean *her* field, for that section with the hardwood, and he would have considered it. But a woman? Nope. She's got an idea in her head about how things are going to be. She's picturing this dream…house'll be here, the picket fence, there, the flowers over yonder… Takes something big to dynamite that picture from a woman's head."

Brandon thought back to how elated Penelope had been that first day. She'd even used the word "dream." Maybe Uncle Jake was right.

But he couldn't just give up on this.

"How serious can she be?" Brandon asked. "How long can she last? Whoever heard of a sculptor living here, anyway?"

"There's that fellow that does chain saw carving. He makes a living at it."

Brandon snorted. "He's retired from the military. Of course he's not starving."

"But this one's got grit."

"Huh?" Brandon saw the frown on his uncle's face and quickly amended the "huh" to "Sir?"

The frown cleared. "Want some apple pie? I bought a frozen one from the store."

Brandon's stomach leapt in anticipation of actual, edible food. "Where is it? I'll get it."

"Fridge. Bottom shelf."

As Brandon retrieved the pie—burnt on one side, but still an improvement over the rice and peas—he prompted his uncle. "What do you mean, she's got grit? You've never met her, have you?"

"Nope. Been here a week now, and she ain't introduced herself. If Geraldine hadn't been doin' so poorly, I'd have gotten round to going over there, being neighborly…"

Brandon dug into the pie and tried not to smile as his uncle digressed into a long and sorry tale about his prize sow.

"So how do you know she's got grit? Penelope, I mean."

His uncle looked startled by Brandon's

change of subject. "You said it yourself. She's got that place livable. She's doing all the work herself. And if she's doing outdoor sculpture, she's got to be handy with a welder. That's a girl who ain't afraid of hard work."

"How do you know about sculpting?"

Uncle Jake waved a hand at the crammed bookshelf on one wall of the dining room. "Some book I read sometime. I forget what. Talked all about it."

"She didn't say anything about welding." But Brandon didn't argue the point.

"She pretty?"

"What?"

"I say, is she pretty?"

An image of tanned legs and dark curly hair spilling over bare shoulders shot into Brandon's mind. "I guess you'd call her pretty."

"Well, then." Uncle Jake beamed. "Maybe she's got a fellow somewhere who wants her back. Or maybe she'll get bored with country boys and head on back to the big city for what she's used to. If she sells out at a decent price, we could get that land back."

A woman like Penelope was attractive

enough to have a long list of guys interested in her. Brandon pushed the plate of pie away and wondered why his uncle's idea didn't cheer him up. Maybe it was because he didn't want to have to wait for Penelope to give up and get lost.

His uncle began clearing the table. Brandon fell into step, not saying anything in response to his uncle's idea.

"What are you so quiet about?" Uncle Jake asked. "Did I say something?"

Brandon dropped the plates into the sink. "No, sir," he replied in a voice he injected with a good measure of cheerfulness.

"Look, Brandon, you gave it your best shot, that land-swapping idea. And there's nothing wrong with hoping she'll give up and go on somewhere else. But you're not dreaming of any shenanigans, are you?"

"Shenanigans?"

"You know, revenge on Murphy. Stealing that land back. Something like that. If I can get my land back fair and square, that's okay. It was my fault I didn't keep that receipt. I should have known better. You pay in cash, you need to be double sure you keep the proof you paid. And yeah, Murphy and Melton took sore advantage of me. Melton is a lying dog, saying I didn't pay that tax debt." Uncle Jake slammed the refrigerator door shut. "But I'll tell you like that doc told me when I had my heart attack over all this. You got to move on, or it will kill you. Toting a grudge will eat you alive."

Brandon said nothing. Let Uncle Jake think what he wanted. He didn't want to admit to Uncle Jake he'd been thinking about how pretty Penelope was or how many lucky guys she had at her fingertips.

No, Brandon wouldn't be one of the guys on Penelope Langston's list. She wasn't the right sort of woman. Couldn't be. Not when she was standing square in the middle of the road to what Brandon was after.

Penelope jabbed the calculator's keypad with the ground-down eraser on her pencil. She'd figured her money three times—and all three times it had agreed.

She'd come up short.

She clenched the pencil, unclenched it, then clenched it again. She glanced over at the single sheet of paper that had laid waste to her plans.

I regret to inform you that we must cancel the commission we'd agreed upon and surrender to you the ten percent deposit already paid. I trust that this comes to you before you've ordered materials...

What a day. First that crazy deputy calling Grandpa a thief, and now *this.* The writing hadn't changed, not in the thirty seconds that had passed since Penelope had last read it.

Fifty grand. Gone up in smoke.

She'd been counting on that money. She'd emptied her checking and savings accounts to pay for the land and the house. Her grandmother had matched her dollar for dollar. An art investment, Grams had called it as she signed the check with a flourish. Penelope had borrowed more money for the studio and renovating the house. That money was spent, and Penelope had borrowed still more money for the studio...

Her brain refused to process anything beyond how this could have happened. She'd played by the rules. She'd got an agreement. She'd done her financial homework.

And yet here she was, caught on the tracks with a mortgage payment bearing down on her—and no way to pay it.

Two months. She had two months before the first payment was due. Penelope said a silent prayer of thanks that she'd taken up the mortgage company's offer for delayed payments.

Theo wound around her legs and yowled for attention. She ignored him. Think. She had to think.

If this company didn't want her sculpture, somebody else would—she'd just have to get out there and sell it. And in the meantime, she'd have to come up with a way to survive without touching the borrowed money in her checking account.

Penelope had survived before. She'd eaten mac and cheese from scratch-and-dent sales and taken on untold numbers of jobs to pay the rent—bartending, car washing, waitressing, even a short stint at a Cineplex, selling popcorn until the smell nauseated her.

One thing she wouldn't do: breathe a word to her parents. She'd learned the hard way that if they even suspected she was going through lean times, they'd be wiring money to her checking account or asking the landlord to check her fridge for food.

She hated the way they'd held her failures over her head as a way to persuade her to join the family business.

Real estate. Land, land, land. Buying, selling, leasing, commercial, residential, option clauses. She'd grown up with it, and it numbed her. When Grandpa Murphy had told her about this land, had suggested she try to buy it and keep it in the family, it had seemed the perfect solution. This property had been the only land she'd ever gotten excited about. Land far enough away that her parents couldn't lie and say, *We stopped by on our way to—*

A knock on the front door cut into Penelope's conflicted thoughts. She frowned and made her way up the hall to the living room.

A glance out the windows told her it was Brandon Wilkes. Her mouth tightened. Wouldn't *he* be glad to know about her commission being canceled?

Penelope threw open the door. "Yes? What do you want now? Me to move to the moon?"

Brandon blinked. "Uh, well...I guess I deserved that. What with my crazy offer. I just—" Brandon broke off. "I came by to apologize. I was taking out my disappointment on you. If...er...if you need a hand with anything, all you have to do is let 'em know at the sheriff's department. I work mostly nights, but they'll find me during the day."

He turned to make his way down the cinder blocks she'd stacked up as impromptu porch steps.

"Wait!"

Brandon paused, turned to her slowly.

"Are you simply being polite? Or do you mean it?"

"Mean what?"

"Your offer." Penelope's mouth went dry. "To help."

"Sure, I mean it. What do you need?"

A wave of uncertainty swamped her. What did she need? A stiff drink, for starters. A sale for a project she'd already ordered the materials for. Any way to save money.

"That barn you were talking about," she said. "The pole barn. Can you help me build it?"

CHAPTER FOUR

"ME? HELP YOU build a barn?"

Brandon's lowered eyebrows and his shocked expression told Penelope all she needed to know.

"Forget it. Just forget it." Her hope turned into a leaden lump of disappointment in her stomach. She turned for the door.

He added, his voice heavy with incredulity, "Let me get this straight. You want a pole barn? And you want me to help you?"

"Well, you needn't be so snippy about it. You were the one who mentioned the pole barn. You sounded nice the other day, before you got all bent out of shape about my grandfather—" She choked off the words, not able to repeat his accusation. Her grandfather a thief. Right. That was about as true as the fraud charges they'd railroaded him with in this federal indictment.

"Yeah, before I got all bent out of shape

about your grandfather being a crook. I take it you don't know him that well."

She bristled. "I know him better than you do. He is my grandfather, after all."

Brandon's lips curled in disdain. "Well, you must see him in a whole different way than I do, then. Maybe with both eyes closed."

She gasped. "I don't have to listen to this!" Penelope headed for the door. She tried to turn the knob, but a tanned hand with long fingers wrapped over hers. She jumped at the contact and looked back over her shoulder.

"Hold it!" Brandon was so close, she could have kissed him. If he wasn't such a jerk.

I don't have time for this, not with a man who thinks my grandfather—I've got a financial disaster raining down on me...

Before she could protest, Brandon stepped back. "Sorry. I didn't want you to go stomping off into the house. Not before I had a chance to, well, show you something."

"Who says I'm interested?"

"Five minutes. That's all I'm asking. It's out here, behind where you've put your house."

Penelope narrowed her eyes and assessed him.

What the heck. What could it hurt? "Let me get my cell phone," she said. If he turned out to be as big a nut as she suspected, at least she could call for help.

Phone in hand, she returned to the porch. "Okay. I'm ready for show-and-tell."

He struck out down the porch and led the way to the back of the house. She had to double-time it to keep up with his long strides over the uneven field. Brandon didn't speak, though, not until he reached a fence splitting her acreage from the neatly harrowed field next to it. The contrast, her untended land adjacent to the cultivated field, couldn't have been more stark.

"This is it? You wanted to show me a fence? It's the land line. Are you going to argue that it's not accurate? Because, let me assure you, I had a new survey done to confirm it," Penelope said.

Brandon put his hands on his hips. "It's in the wrong place, all right. It shouldn't be there at all."

Penelope rolled her eyes. Not more about this land business. Grandpa Murphy said people were out to get him, and this guy was proof of that.

"I bought this land at a public auction. The bank loaned me money on it. I can prove the title is clear."

"Well, let me tell you a little about this land." Brandon couldn't seem to get his next words out. Penelope saw raw pain in his eyes.

It caught her short. She didn't turn and walk off as she'd intended to. Instead, she waited to see what he would finally say.

"My uncle farmed this land. This was the first acreage he ever owned." Brandon swept an arm over the expanse of the field. He pointed out Penelope's house. "Where your house is now, that's where he first plowed, the day he bought the land. You ought to hear him tell the story. He didn't even have a tractor to plow with, so he borrowed—"

He didn't finish, but looked embarrassed. "Anyway, like I said, this land has been Uncle Jake's since he was just out of school. And then a couple of years ago—" Now Brandon clenched his jaw, along with his fists.

"He needed the money, so he took what

Grandpa Murphy offered him," Penelope supplied. "Look, I'm sorry—"

Brandon exploded. "He needed the money because Murphy defrauded a bunch of landowners in this county. His brother-in-law—I guess that's your family, too, huh?"

"Uh, no. Grandpa Murphy divorced my grandmother years ago and he remarried. Why am I explaining this to you? My grandfather is not a crook—"

"Tell that to the federal investigators itching to indict him." Before she could protest, he said, "Murphy and the tax commissioner, who just happened to be his wife's brother, handpicked a few of the old farmers who tended to pay with cash. It was common knowledge in this county. When the tax commissioner suddenly turned up with a tax notice in his hand, my Uncle Jake couldn't produce a paid receipt. That's when Murphy jumped in with his oh-so-convenient 'help.' It nearly killed Uncle Jake to lose this land. But what choice did he have?"

"Forgive me if I find it hard to believe your version of events." Penelope gazed around the open land and saw how carefully it had been tended on the other side of the new fence. She thought about how proud she'd been of her purchase. How hard it must have been for the person who had lost it.

Sympathy softened her voice as she said, "Listen, I know this must be difficult for you. I think it's admirable that you're trying to look out for your uncle."

"This fence…I plowed a tractor over this land many a day. I never dreamed…" Brandon shook his head. "My uncle's not in the best of health. He's old, and he lost half of his farm to Murphy. Before then, he and I were partners. He still farms—well, I do most of the heavy work—but it's just really small-time. See, this summer Murphy planted dodder vine in Uncle Jake's cotton, and he didn't have crop insurance."

Penelope folded her arms across her chest. "Grandpa Murphy's told me all about the way the federal government is saying that he's some sort of criminal mastermind, all because some noxious weed got brought in by a drifter from Texas."

Brandon's chuckle was bitter. "Yeah, right. I'm sure the way Murphy tells it, he didn't have a thing to do with either coercing JT Griggs into bringing dodder vine here or swindling Uncle Jake. But let me tell you something—Richard Murphy's no sweet old grandfather. He's always working the angles."

Brandon's tone was so scornful that Penelope ignored his yammering about people she didn't know and concentrated instead on the situation at hand. "Okay, so let's use logic on this. Why on earth would my grandfather go to all that trouble? Land's land, right? Why would he risk going to jail to get this particular tract?"

Brandon lifted his shoulders. "I gave up trying to figure out Murphy a long time ago. But my idea is that pond over there."

"The pond?" Penelope squinted. She shaded her eyes and took in the large pond that stretched back from the land's dip toward the creek and an old abandoned rail spur. "What good would that do him?"

"Irrigation. That's a natural pond, and there's a stream that ends up in a small creek. It's what my uncle used to irrigate this section of his farm. Your grandfather used it for a water supply for his migrant workers and to deprive my uncle of a way to water his crops."

"So that's what this is about?" Penelope compressed her lips and kicked at the dirt. "You want the water? Fine, run irrigation from it. I'm not using it. But a piece of advice—next time you want to sweet-talk someone into letting you access her water, don't accuse her grandfather of being a crook."

"It's not just the water. I want the land. The land is ours, well, Uncle Jake's. I want it back for him. I tried to buy this land for him at auction, and *you* ran the cost up. I should have known Murphy had something to do with it. You certainly don't need thirty acres of prime farmland."

She stood stock-still, the solution to her money crunch within her grasp. "I don't need all this land, you're right. If you want it so badly, then maybe we can work out a deal. I'll sell you all but, say, five acres."

If she'd expected Brandon to extend a tanned forearm in a glad handshake and say *Sold!* he didn't. Instead he muttered under his breath and shook his head.

"Hey, you want it. I'm offering. I'll even—"

Penelope shrugged. "I'm fair. I'll sell it for what I paid for it. You can't beat that, can you?"

Brandon's eyes darkened. "What you paid for it was at least twice what Murphy paid my uncle. He paid him, to the dime, the taxes and penalties and interest the county said he owed."

"Well, why didn't your uncle fight it?"

"He did. How do you think he lost what he did? Rotten lawyers took his savings and then in the end, he didn't have proof that he'd paid. My uncle's—" Brandon winced. "Ah, forget it. I thought I could make you understand."

"Brandon..." Maybe it was the way his pain and loss seemed at odds with his big frame. But something made her reach out and touch his arm. "I can't pretend to understand what your uncle went through. But I know how I feel, seeing my grandfather losing all his land and in so much legal trouble. I know how helpless I feel. It must be twice as bad for you."

"I do feel helpless. I want to fix it, you know?" Brandon pushed his fingers through

ditions. One, you have to sell it to me for fair market value *before* you ran up the price—that's all the bank would lend me. And two, that not one dime of my money goes to Richard Murphy."

"Are you out of your tree? You can't tell me what I do with the money after you get the land, any more than I can tell you what to do with the land."

"So I'm right, then? That's why you need the money? For Murphy?"

"No, I need the money to survive on, to pay my bills. But if my grandfather needs help, you can bet I'll share what I have. He's old, Brandon, and frail and I don't want him in prison."

"Frail? Richard Murphy frail? He's healthy as a horse—no, make that an ox. You make him sound like he's on his last legs." Brandon narrowed his eyes. "No. As bad as I want this land back in my family, I will not pay Richard Murphy, not a red cent. And I sure won't add to his legal defense fund. He may be your grandfather, but he belongs in jail.

And I'll do everything I can to make sure he ends up there."

With that, he stalked back toward the house and his truck, leaving Penelope speechless.

CHAPTER FIVE

BRANDON HADN'T REALIZED how tight his fists were until his knuckles started aching. He stood by his truck and sucked in a purposeful breath. In. Out. In again. Slow exhale.

Better. The idea that he'd let one cent of his money go to Richard Murphy's lawyers...

No. Calm down. Think.

The vinyl seat crackled under him as he slammed the door with one hand and punched in Ryan MacIntosh's number on his cell phone with the other.

"Ryan? You got a few minutes? If you do, I'm on the way over."

His best friend didn't hesitate. "Come on. Mee-Maw's got lunch on the table and Becca can put out another plate. We've got Sean Courtland here, too, so we can all hear what he has to say about the investigation."

Brandon didn't know what cheered him up more. Was it the idea of Ryan's grandmother's legendary meals? Or the possibility that in the course of the dinner, Sean, the FBI agent who'd been investigating Murphy, might have news? Ostensibly, Sean was there to gather more information from one of the government's star witnesses, Ryan's grandmother. Sean, though, didn't mind giving the latest to Brandon. Sean would wink and chalk it up to inter-agency cooperation.

During the ten minutes or so it took him to drive over to the MacIntosh farm, Brandon managed to gain a more positive attitude. Murphy was going down, and soon. Maybe Sean was there to tell them that the federal indictment, which had already dragged on for a couple of months without materializing, was about to be handed down.

Besides, Brandon could never come to the MacIntosh farm without remembering how Ryan and Becca, Ryan's new wife, had finally put Murphy in the government's crosshairs. And if that wasn't cause to celebrate, he didn't know what was.

The smell of country-fried steak and gravy enveloped him as Mee-Maw opened the door for him. Her lined face was wreathed in smiles.

"Well, if it ain't my favorite deputy! C'mon in, Brandon! We've got plenty. Wash up and go fix your plate."

He heard the hubbub of conversation at the kitchen table as he scrubbed his hands in the bathroom sink.

If only I could wash away the memory of Penelope Langston defending her grandfather. It just went to show that you couldn't judge a person by how she looked, no matter how pretty.

Penelope's dark eyes, snapping with fire, came back to him. She was as easy to read as a mood ring: when she was mad, her eyes went almost black. Otherwise they were warm and brown, like melted caramel.

At the table, Brandon pulled out a ladder-back chair and settled in it.

Becca grinned. "Now this is better than any lunch in town, isn't it?" she asked as she passed him a bowl of creamed potatoes. "I swear, Mee-Maw's cooking was half the reason I married Ryan."

Brandon chuckled. He knew better than

that. It didn't take a rocket scientist to see that Ryan was head over heels for Becca—and vice versa. He wondered if, when they had kids, the children would inherit Becca's blond hair or Ryan's red.

Sean Courtland lifted up a big fluffy biscuit and inspected it. "Ma'am, these are so good that I might have to report it as a gourmet gift. It's lucky this is my day off and I'm not on duty."

Mee-Maw beamed. "Aw, just a little something I threw together. Next time I'll cook you some good fried chicken. Brandon, how's your Uncle Jake doing?"

Brandon's creamed potatoes suddenly looked a lot less appetizing. He pushed the food listlessly on his plate. "He's okay, I guess. Same as always. Impatient to hear what the latest is on Murphy."

Sean swallowed the bite of biscuit he'd just taken before answering. "U.S. attorney still wants more. You know these guys, they don't indict anything less than a slam-dunk case. They don't want to sully their conviction rate with a not-guilty verdict."

"How much more do they need? I thought

we'd given them enough for their slam-dunk conviction. If I can't see Murphy go to jail for swindling Uncle Jake, I want to at least see the feds take him down for his crop insurance fraud." Brandon set the gravy boat down harder than he should have, netting a scolding look from Mee-Maw. He double-checked to make sure no gravy had splashed on her tablecloth.

"Brandon's right," Ryan said. "They've got the crop insurance adjustor, they've got, what, two of the farmers who were conspiring with Murphy. They've got JT Griggs willing to testify that Murphy made him bring in the dodder vine with intent to defraud the government."

At the mention of JT's name, Sean frowned. "JT has a credibility issue, guys, and you know it. He's served time. I think he's telling the truth, the U.S. attorney thinks he is…but will the jury? And so that's why they want more guys to plead out and agree to testify against Murphy. It will happen. The big news I wanted to tell you—Becca, you'll really get excited about this—we've run down the guy who attacked Becca in her motel room. And his shyster lawyer is about to sign off on a plea agreement."

"So that's another nail in Murphy's coffin?" Brandon's appetite came back with renewed gusto. "The guy is willing to say Murphy put him up to it?"

"Well, no," Sean conceded. "He's saying it was the brainstorm of that other farmer, Tate. But if we put pressure on Tate, then Tate will roll over on Murphy."

Brandon chewed on the steak as he considered this and decided, if it wasn't perfect, at least it was a move in the right direction. "That will complicate Murphy's legal woes. Hey, did you guys know Penelope Langston is Murphy's granddaughter?"

Becca's and Ryan's mouths dropped open, but Brandon noted Sean didn't look as surprised.

"Yeah. We'd come up on that in our investigation. She's some sort of artist, I think, from Oregon, but she'd been living in New York. Apparently she came down here to offer moral support."

"She's willing to offer him more than moral support. She had the nerve to offer to sell me the land—Uncle Jake's land, mind you—to raise money for Murphy." Brandon took a swig of iced tea that did nothing to cool off his temper.

"She said that?" Becca's eyes rounded. "That's… that's brassy."

"Well, she didn't exactly put it that way. She's a sculptor, and she had this big sale for, I kid you not, three pieces of stainless steel welded together, but it fell through. So now she needs money. I just didn't want any of my money ending up in Richard Murphy's hands. When she wouldn't agree to that stipulation, I told her no. I guess the apple doesn't fall too far from the tree."

Ryan nodded as he passed the tall pitcher of iced tea to Becca. "Sounds like you can wait her out, then. If she needs money, then maybe you can pick up the land in a foreclosure deal."

"That's what I was thinking," Brandon agreed. "It galls me to even think about Uncle Jake being forced to sell to Murphy in the first place."

"I'm still working with the state's revenue department on that, Brandon," Becca said.

"They're saying now that the forced sales of both this property and your uncle's might not be legal. So Uncle Jake might get the land after all."

"Now that's more like it!" Brandon rubbed his hands together.

"If the title's in question..." Sean trailed off in thought.

"Yeah?" Brandon prompted.

"Well, I was thinking of adverse possession. If the title's in question, and you cultivate the land for seven years, it's yours anyway."

"You mean, just act like it's mine and it turns into my land?"

"Yeah. The key is the action has to be hostile, without permission from the landowner, but the landowner in turn has to not put a stop to it. The law says that if the landowner doesn't care about someone else improving or cultivating land, the land should belong to the one making the investment of money and labor. Of course, seven years is a long time to wait."

"Maybe by then Penelope Langston will be gone," Brandon said.

Mee-Maw cleared her throat, and the group of them turned toward her at the head of the table.

"Mee-Maw? You have something on your mind?" Ryan asked.

Ryan's grandmother tore at a biscuit in her fingers, shredding it absentmindedly. "I remember that girl. Not well, mind you. She hasn't been around here in years. Why, I guess she was seven or eight the last time she came to visit. That little one—Penelope, you say? Not big as a minute, and always drawing. I kept her some, that last time, because of course the likes of Murphy couldn't be bothered with entertaining his granddaughter. She had a good heart, was right faithful about helping me nurse a calf and see to the chickens."

"So what are you trying to say, Mee-Maw?" Brandon asked. "That she can't have grown up to be like Murphy if she was willing to help you bottle-feed a calf?"

Mee-Maw stretched out a gnarled finger and shook it in Brandon's direction. "Young man, people aren't always what they seem at first blush. Yes, sir, most times they are, and you best not expect much more out of 'em, but people's hearts don't change. I expect it's Penelope's heart that's telling her to look after her grandfather, even if he is a black-hearted crook. I'd be more worried about her if she didn't have some speck of caring for the man. So don't you be too hard on her."

Brandon took the chastisement on the chin. But he reserved judgment. How could anyone be fooled by the likes of Richard Murphy?

CHAPTER SIX

"GRANDPA! No! What do you think you're doing?"

Just inside Grandpa Murphy's kitchen door, Penelope made a grab for the glazed doughnut in her grandfather's hand. Grandpa Murphy snatched it back just out of her reach, a scowl on his face.

"Penny-girl! It'll be all right—I'll take an extra insulin shot. No big deal."

But Penelope closed the gap between them, confiscated the doughnut and the eleven still in the box. "I'll just go put this in my car where they won't tempt you. Grandpa, you know you've been having trouble with your sugar levels. You have to—"

"Have absolutely no fun, that's what I have to do. Penny-girl, what's one little ol' doughnut when I might be behind bars soon? They're circling in for the kill, the lot of 'em."

Penelope wrapped her arm around her

grandfather's too-big middle and gave him an encouraging hug. "You are not supposed to be worrying, remember? You told me the doctor said that stress complicated regulating your blood-sugar levels. Those lawyers of yours will do their job. There is such a thing as reasonable doubt and innocent before proven guilty."

Grandpa Murphy hugged her back. "You are a sight for sore eyes. Sorry I'm such a sourpuss, girl."

Penelope felt a tug on the box in her hand. Grandpa stepped back, a doughnut triumphantly in his grasp and took a quick bite out of it.

"You are absolutely incorrigible, did you know that? Who brought you those doughnuts, anyway? Now we've got to fuss with the test strips and check to see how much insulin you need, and you'll probably need a shot."

He waved away her concerns and took another bite. "And you tell me not to worry. You're a fine one to be talking. I bought my own doughnuts, thank you very much. Sit down here at the table. You know how many years I wanted you around so I could have the pleasure of you just dropping in for an unexpected visit?"

His words blew away her aggravation. In the scheme of things, what was one doughnut as long as she could make sure his blood sugar was okay before she left? She'd missed him for so long. If only her mother could have gotten along with Grandpa Murphy. If only Mom had given him a chance.

They sat down at Grandpa Murphy's kitchen table and she watched as he savored the doughnut, licking the last of the glaze off his fingertips. "Bum pancreas. Don't ever let your pancreas go to pot, girl. Worst thing in the world."

"Well, not the worst, surely."

"No, I'd guess federal prison is worse."

Penelope's heart squeezed in her chest. "Your lawyers will help you, Grandpa. You're not going to prison. You didn't do anything wrong, right? They don't put innocent people in prison."

"They do if they're out for blood. And they are out for blood—mine. If they'll believe that JT, a farmhand with no high school degree, somebody who's been in the clink before, I don't have a chance. I might as well eat that whole box of doughnuts."

"Are we feeling sorry for ourselves today?" Penelope met his eyes pointedly.

Grandpa Murphy's mouth pulled down even more, but then he lifted his chin. "Forget them. I'm not going to let them get me down. Cheer me up, Penelope, tell me something to get my mind off my troubles."

"Uh…" She thought about the reason she'd come over, to ask about Brandon Wilkes's intense hatred of her grandfather.

"That sculpture you're working on. You got started on it yet?"

Ouch. Another tender point. She hadn't intended on telling him about the cancelled commission. "Well. About that. I've had a bit of a setback. The company has changed its mind."

"About buying it? Just as well you hadn't got started on it then. Tell 'em to go jump in a lake somewhere. Bad break for you, Penny-girl, but I'll bet you'll get everything figured out. You're a Murphy, after all, and Murphys land on their feet."

She reached over and patted his hand. "I'm

still going to do it. Don't worry. I'm not giving up yet. But thanks, Grandpa, for not going all ballistic on me. Mom would have insisted I turn everything back over to the bank, pack up and come home."

"Your mother is nothing if she's not a Chicken Little. Always in an uproar about something." He leaned back in his chair, the back of it creaking under his weight. "So what are your plans? You have enough money to make it?"

"I'm…I'm not sure. Haven't landed on my feet yet, but I'm working on it." She tried to inject a cheerful, confident note in her voice.

"I might have just the thing for you, then. If you don't need that entire tract of land, you interested in selling part of it?"

She cocked her head to one side and stared at him. "Is it something in the air?"

"What do you mean?"

Penelope hesitated. "Brandon Wilkes came—"

Grandpa Murphy scowled and banged a fist on the table.

Penelope laughed uneasily. "I take it you

don't have any more warm, fuzzy feelings for him than he does for you."

"Busybody deputy. It was him and Ryan MacIntosh and that Becca Reynolds MacIntosh hooked up with—all of them got me in this jam I'm in. They'd like nothing more than to see me rot behind bars, Penelope. You stay away from them."

"That won't be a problem. I've not been the one looking for Brandon, that's for sure." The dark expression on Brandon's good-looking face came back fresh and clear. He'd been so self-righteous about the whole thing, as though there were no doubt that her grandfather had orchestrated the loss of his uncle's land.

He really believed it, too. Penelope had seen the way his expression had softened when he talked about his uncle, had seen pain in his eyes. That pain had driven her here, to be sure that she wasn't profiting off something that hadn't been on the up-and-up.

"Grandpa Murphy?" Penelope struggled to couch the question in a nonaccusatory way. "About how you got the Wilkes property…"

Grandpa's lips thinned. "Told you, girl.

I told you all that when I first called you about the banks calling in all my notes and my entire place going on the auction block. Lousy banks, getting all my money. I got the land when Jake Wilkes's old tax debt finally caught up with him. A man doesn't think he has to pay taxes and then makes up all kinds of stories about how he paid it. Well, why can't he produce proof, I say?"

"Brandon said there were other—"

"You listening to that Brandon Wilkes? You believe that lug of a deputy over me? Your own flesh and blood?" he thundered, his face turning purple.

Penelope held up a hand. "Whoa, calm down, Grandpa. Of course I believe you. I wanted to be sure, that's all."

She could see a storm of emotions swirl over him, but finally his expression settled into an uneasy calm. "Yeah. Yeah. That Brandon can spin a sad tale, that's for sure. I can see why you felt the need to ask, although, I can't lie. It cuts that you doubted me, your own grandfather."

"I'm sorry, Grandpa. I meant…I wasn't questioning…well, I guess I was, wasn't I?"

Penelope chuckled, but that didn't ease the tension.

"It's okay, Penelope. I understand. But listen, about your money problems."

The abrupt shift in topic confused her for a moment. "That's okay, Grandpa, I'll figure—"

"No, no. I want to hook you up with some people, some folks who will give you good money for your land. They've been after it for a while. Before the banks started calling in their notes, I was about to sell the land you've got now to these people."

"If they wanted the land, why didn't they bid against me at the auction?"

"Didn't know about it. It all happened so fast. Penny-girl, I hope you never have to see all you worked for being bid off on the auction block. It's a horrible thing."

She wrapped her fingers around his again and squeezed. The twist of his lips reminded her of Brandon's when he'd tried to explain his uncle's loss. "I feel really awful, Grandpa, that I managed to profit off your misfortune."

He pulled his hand from hers and pressed his fingertips to his eyes. "Well, if I had to lose it all, I'm glad some of it went to you. That's why I told you. You're family, Penny-girl, and I knew you'd want to help out. I knew you wouldn't want to see everything I'd worked for gone."

"I do want to help." Penelope dropped her gaze from him and busied herself with straightening her grandfather's bottles of medicine in the center of the kitchen table. Did he have to take so much?

"Then talk to these people. They have this solid-waste facility company, based out of Florida. They do all this gee-whiz stuff to garbage and recycle it, all with robots and stuff. Hardly a human hand touches it."

"Solid waste?" Penelope set down the bottle in her hand. "Oh, Grandpa, I don't know. That doesn't sound like—"

"It's all real, what do you call it? Green? Keeps it out of landfills and stuff. I figured that'd be right up your alley, Penny-girl, as big on the environment as you are. And these guys are so hot for it that they're willing to pay three times the market value. Why do you think I didn't tell 'em about the auction? I figured you and me, we could sell it together." He leaned forward in his chair, his face alight with excitement. "And then…well, no lie, Penny, I need every dime I can get for those vultures I call lawyers. I can't face going to jail. You said you wanted to help me."

Penclope struggled for the words to tell him no without hurting him. Solid waste? A company that, from the sound of it, used hardly any employees?

"Don't say no. If you can't say yes right now, say you'll think about it, okay? Don't say no," Grandpa Murphy urged her. "Just think about it. There's no rush. No rush at all."

"I offered to sell to Brandon," she confessed.

Again he slammed a hand down on the table. With visible effort, he reined his temper back in. "He can't beat this deal, Penny-girl. And remember, you can't trust him. Not one whit. He's the reason I'm in this mess to begin with."

CHAPTER SEVEN

"You're up to something."

Uncle Jake's statement stopped Brandon in his tracks as he was coming out of his uncle's toolshed. He looked down at the stakes and twine he held. His guilt made them feel poker-hot in his hands.

"No. I'm just helping out a neighbor," Brandon said.

Uncle Jake narrowed his eyes and, with the hand not holding a bucket, shifted his cap. It was a move Brandon knew well, a gesture that signaled Uncle Jake's keen mind was in full gear, calculating angles and motives. When Brandon had been in high school, that cap-shifting move meant Brandon was about to get busted, whether it was for sneaking out to join his buddies at the river or for a less-than-stellar grade he hadn't told his mother about.

This time was no exception. "Hmm. That

there is my surveying twine and my line level. And my stakes. Looks like you're all set to help someone stake out a foundation."

"A cement slab for a pole barn, actually."

Uncle Jake got that "ah-ha" glint in his eyes. "Penelope Langston's barn? You gonna help her with that after all?"

"Yes, sir."

"Mind if I ask why you're all het up to help her? A mighty quick change of heart, just saying."

"I could say that's how you and Mama raised me." Brandon fidgeted with the spool of twine in hope that his hedged words would distract his uncle.

It didn't happen.

"Right. You all of a sudden remembering your raisings, and all that. Way I see it, it's got to be one of two things." Uncle Jake set the bucket by his feet and propped himself against a nearby fence post. "Either she's prettier than you've let on, or else you're making some other kind of move on her. 'Cause the Brandon I know doesn't forgive and forget and build pole barns."

"I guess I should have asked, Uncle Jake,

if you minded me helping her, but you should know, it's not—"

"Mind? Son, that land is gone. It's not ours anymore. Not one smidge of it. I knew that the day I realized I couldn't find that paid receipt for my taxes. My mistake. My carelessness played right into Murphy's and Melton's hands. They tried it on a bunch of us, and the ones who'd kept their receipts—well, they've still got their land, now don't they?"

"But Uncle Jake, if it hadn't have been for Murphy, you would—"

"Uh-huh, you are up to some scheming. I didn't think you had gotten rid of all that vinegar you were spewing."

Brandon shifted his hold on the twine, stakes and the level. He looked down at them and leaned the stakes against the shed. What would he accomplish by helping Penelope? "I started thinking. She's got money troubles. She won't be able to hold on to the land that much longer, and we'll be able to buy it. Plus, Becca MacIntosh is still working on proving the original sale wasn't legal, so it may revert back to you without a penny being swapped. And, worse comes to worst, there's the pos-

his hair then dropped his hand. He shrugged. "I'm sorry I wasted your time."

"Maybe you haven't. I'm serious about selling part of the land." Penelope couldn't meet his eyes as she recalled the letter she'd received earlier in the day. "Let's just say I'm in sudden need of money."

"But—" Brandon frowned.

"But what?"

"What about your sculpture? I thought all you had to do was weld three pieces of stainless steel together and, presto, you were fifty grand richer."

She sighed. "They canceled the commission. I've already bought the materials, and if I returned them, I'd have to pay shipping and a hefty restocking fee. So I'm going to build it anyway. But I need money. You want the land. Why not make everybody happy?"

Brandon nodded, and she could see from his expression he was considering it. She clenched her fists in anticipation, slipped her index finger across her middle finger.

Please, please, please, buy this land.

But then his eyes lit on the fence again, and his expression hardened. "Okay. On two con-

sibility of that adverse possession Sean was talking about. One way or another, we'll get it back, Uncle Jake. Why shouldn't I go ahead and start improving the land? We can always use another barn."

Uncle Jake's face creased in a frown. "Brandon, that most certainly is *not* the way your mama and I raised you. Your mama would be spinning in her grave like a chicken on a spit if she could hear you. You know how bad it hurt me to lose that land."

"Which is why I'm trying to get it back."

"And there's that girl, ain't hurt so much as a fly, and you're scheming to cheat her out of the land same as Murphy cheated me out of it. I tell you, that land is cursed, Brandon. You'd do well to leave it alone." Uncle Jake shook his head and looked off into the distance.

After a moment of silence that Brandon couldn't figure out how to fill, his uncle snatched up the bucket and brushed past him. "I expect, though, as hardheaded as you are, you'll have to figure that one out for yourself. But don't say I didn't warn you when this comes back to bite you."

AT THE SOUND of a vehicle coming along the driveway, Penelope looked up from the hole she was digging with her handheld spade to see a familiar dust-covered truck and knew Brandon was at the wheel. She tensed. What could he want now?

She rose to her feet. If he was here to malign her grandfather, he could hit the road.

Brandon had just slid one booted foot out of his truck door and onto her driveway when she rounded the front of his truck.

"Back to insult my family some more? Or are you still insisting I should give this land to you?"

He paused, one hand on the open window. Then he reached behind him and pulled out a bundle of stakes and a ball of twine.

"Oh, that's rich," she said, recognizing the items for what they were. "You're already acting like it's your land!"

"Whoa." Brandon eased around the truck door and slammed it shut. "Can't you even give a guy a chance to apologize?"

"Apologize?" Penelope didn't bother to keep her suspicion out of her voice.

"Yeah. Okay, so I got a little hot under the collar. I'm not usually like that. It's just this land." Brandon clamped his mouth shut. He started again. "Anyway, it's like Uncle Jake pointed out a few minutes ago. It's his fault, ultimately. He was the one who couldn't produce the receipt that proved he'd paid the taxes. My uncle's never been much for paperwork, and this time it cost him. So about how I acted—to, er, make it up to you, I thought I'd help you out with your barn."

"You what?" Her hold on the spade loosened and she dropped it.

"The pole barn. The one that you asked me to help you with?"

To cover her confusion, she knelt to retrieve the spade. "Why?" Penelope asked.

"Like I said. I want to make it up to you. The way I reacted."

She straightened, realizing how tall he was when she only came to mid-chest. It was a very broad, very well built chest, which stretched the cotton knit T-shirt tight. "Look, it was stupid and more than a little insensitive of me to ask you for help. I appreciate the gesture, but I'll figure something out."

"What are you doing over there? Planting flowers? It's late in the year for flowers. I know it's still hot now, but fall's first hard frost won't be too much longer."

She followed his gaze to her garden plot. "No. Winter vegetables. I'm going to build a cold frame to go over them."

"Not much of a garden if you're doing it with that thing." Brandon glanced dismissively at the spade in her hand. "Why don't you let me bring my uncle's tractor over here and I'll break you up a proper garden spot, one big enough to do you some good?"

"This is enough for me. It's called square-foot gardening."

"Humph. This I've got to see." Brandon took long strides over to the plot, with its grids laid out in string. "Two winter squash plants? That bit of spinach? You must have the appetite of a bird."

"No, see, you use the space over and over. Once a square has produced all it will, you pull that plant up and plant something else."

"I still think you'd be better off with a bigger garden."

"This is actually a much better, more intensive use of the land. It's kinder to the environment, doesn't require as much fertilizer. And you do it all organically."

"Right." The corners of Brandon's mouth twitched. "Well, if you change your mind, we've got enough time to break you a bigger spot for, say, turnip or mustard greens."

"Turnips. Those are the things with the purple roots? Or am I thinking of rutabagas?"

"No, you're right, turnips are purple. But you eat the tops, too."

"Oh. Like spinach?"

"Yeah, only cooked. Turnips are too peppery to eat raw in a salad."

Standing here with him, talking about gardens and vegetables, she'd found herself getting lost in his easy, open grin and pulled herself up short. Her grandfather's warning rang in her ears.

What if he was here to buy the land? She'd agreed to it, but now Grandpa Murphy had asked her to at least talk to these solid-waste guys. Truth be told, she'd rather sell to Brandon, if he wouldn't put ludicrous strings on the way she spent her money.

"Here I am. Ready to help you get the barn site prepped for a concrete slab. Or if you're really tight on funds, you can keep a dirt floor in it for the time being, have the concrete poured later."

"I don't know what to say."

"Just tell me where you want the barn. I'll lay it out and then I'll get the FFA members to help me put it up."

"FFA members?"

"Uh, Future Farmers of America? Well, that's what they used to be called, but now I don't think the initials really stand for anything. Anyway, it's a high school agricultural class and a club, and they get extra credit for projects like this. I'm one of the community advisors, so I can get the ag teacher to lend us some young strong backs."

Penelope shook her head. "What's in it for you?"

Brandon reacted as though he'd been slapped. "Nothing."

"I didn't mean to insult you, but you have to admit it's perplexing. One day you're here, saying you'll do anything to see my grandfather in jail and that this land is really yours, and the next day you're here offering to help me build a barn?"

"Your *grandfather,*" Brandon said between gritted teeth, "is a thief and an extortionist and his ethics leave a lot to be desired. If you want my help, you'd best not remind me why I don't have this land to begin with."

"Fine. Surely there are other people around here who know how to build a pole barn. And maybe my being Richard Murphy's granddaughter won't matter so much to them." Penelope folded her arms across her chest.

She could admit to herself—but only to herself—that she was being childish. But Brandon's high-handedness irritated her.

He shrugged but his eyes belied his indifference. "Suits me. But I wouldn't bank on finding anybody in this town who feels warm and fuzzy toward anyone related to Richard Murphy. He stepped on a lot of people on his way up, and he can take a lot of his buddies with him on his way down. Plus, I'm the one who can help you get that cheap labor you were after. But it's up to you. If I were really as bad as you're thinking, I wouldn't lift a finger. I'd just wait for the foreclosure sale. Or for you to get even more desperate."

Her anger melted away. She *was* being

childish. He'd offered to help, and she was only reminding him of all the reasons he'd be better off not helping her.

"I'm sorry. You're not catching me at my best today. Can we start over?" She stuck out her hand. "Hi, I'm your new neighbor, Penelope Langston, and I'd like to invite you to a barn raising. That's right, isn't it? A barn raising?"

Brandon's tense expression dissolved into amusement and he clasped her hand in his. "I guess. We don't worry too much around here about how we say things."

He didn't let go of her hand, just held it snugly in his and gave it a squeeze. When he did release her fingers, she missed the comfort that squeeze had given her.

"Did you mean what you said the other day? That I could use the land and the irrigation pond?" Brandon asked.

For a moment, suspicion niggled at her. But she had offered and, even if her grandfather would explode—it was juvenile to say no. The man was offering to help her with her studio, which in turn would help her generate revenue.

"Of course. I'm not using it. I'll certainly rent it to you. I do, however, object to things like tobacco being planted on it."

Brandon threw his head back in a belly laugh. "You'd negotiate a stickup guy out of his gun, wouldn't you? You just don't give up. Relax. I don't grow tobacco or any other thing you could find objectionable. It's not even the right time of year for that. You don't know beans about farming, do you?"

"A country girl I'm not. It would, um, be pushing it to insist you use organic principles?"

"Yeah. It would. But if you can figure out a way to make that pay, I'm all for it."

Penelope bit back her speech about pay it now or pay it later and committed herself to finding information on the evils of pesticides and chemical fertilizers so she could educate him instead. "Okay, then. What's next?"

"What's next is we pick out a spot for your barn. I talk to the FFA instructor for you, and I figure out a list of materials we'll need to build this. And then you really get to see a barn raising."

"Oh, I'll help. I'm stronger than I look," Penelope said.

Brandon nodded. "I remember that tae-kwon-whatever-it-was on the highway. You nearly had me on the ground. You bet you'll invest sweat equity in this project. You'll discover muscles you never knew you had."

Her eyes fell on his biceps, bunched up under the cotton of his T-shirt. Suddenly, she couldn't wait to see him break a sweat himself.

CHAPTER EIGHT

BRANDON STOOD by the tarp-covered stack of materials for Penelope's pole barn and wished he didn't feel so conflicted.

If he played his cards right, he could give this land back to Uncle Jake tied up in a bow. For now, with the rental agreement he'd worked out with Penelope, he and Uncle Jake had the right to treat the land like it was theirs again.

So why did he feel as though he was a conniving jerk?

It *was* his land—well, Uncle Jake's. And Murphy had stolen it. He'd most likely roped Penelope into buying it, and while Brandon hated that Penelope would be a loser in all this, she *would,* ultimately, lose.

Brandon wasn't cheating Penelope out of anything, because the land hadn't ever been Murphy's to sell. If she hadn't come to Georgia with her high-priced lawyers bidding up the auction price, that land would have been back in the Wilkes's hands.

But no, she had. And because of that… Brandon looked out over the property and saw the ugly, hateful fence running through the middle of it, like a surgeon's scar. It didn't need to be there. It shouldn't have ever been put there. And if Brandon had anything to do with it, it was coming down.

The ends justified the means, right? And that's why he was here doing something supremely stupid, putting something fairly permanent on land designed for growing things. A barn? On prime cropland? And for a sculpture she didn't even have a buyer for?

The day of the barn raising had dawned crisp and clear, blue skies dotted with the white clouds only early October in Georgia could give you. No more aluminum-gray skies obscured with haze from the summer heat. Autumn in Georgia—if you could call eighty degrees fall weather—had arrived.

So had Penelope. She bounced from the house toward the barn site, looking more like the girl he'd first met than the suspicious specimen he'd recently been tangling with.

"Where are they? I thought they'd be here by now!"

"Relax," he told her. "It's only eight o'clock."

"You really think we can get this done today?"

"The big part of it, hopefully. I'll have to come back with some friends of mine and put the roof on. It's too much of a liability to put schoolkids up that high."

Before she could ask the next question he knew was coming, a beat-up truck, more body filler and primer than paint on its fenders, pulled up beside Brandon's. His heart sank.

"Aw, no. What's Uncle Jake doing here?"

"Your uncle?"

"Yeah. Hold on. I hope those hogs of his aren't out again."

Uncle Jake's easy steps out of the truck and around to the back of it signaled no urgency, though. He reached over and fished for something. Brandon couldn't tell what it was.

"Uncle Jake?" Brandon called. "What's wrong?"

"Can't find my hammer, blast it. No, wait, there she is." Uncle Jake stuck the hammer in his belt loop with a satisfied pat. "A man can't show up at a barn raising without his best hammer."

"You're here to help?"

"You betcha. I told Geraldine she was in charge of the hogs and not to be lettin' 'em pull any Houdini tricks until I could get back. Fat lot of good that'll do."

He looked past Brandon, raised a hand in a wave and started walking toward Penelope. "How-do. Jake Wilkes. I'm this 'un's uncle, practically raised him, so if he gets fresh with you, you tell me about it. I'll put a kink in his tail, for sure."

Another truck pulled up, this one in better shape. Out clambered Ryan MacIntosh, along with Becca and Mee-Maw. Before they could even shout a hello, Brandon saw more trucks making the turn into the driveway.

He felt his small amount of control of the day slipping away. "Uncle Jake, you didn't…"

"Oh, I told a few people. Neighborly thing to do, wasn't it? Since you are being so neighborly." Uncle Jake raised his eyebrows, daring Brandon to challenge him. "Besides, we haven't had a proper barn raisin' since I was…hmm—" he winked at Penelope "—still young enough to cut the muster."

Brandon tried to squelch the groan working its way out of him. No telling what Uncle Jake had told everyone to get them to pitch in. He'd probably said that Brandon had a new girlfriend who was in dire need of rescuing. This many people, along with a full crew of FFA students, would be a circus.

And that was the least of his objections. This was his plan, but he didn't feel right about dragging his uncle into it. Or anybody else, for that matter.

Penelope, however, showed nothing short of delight. She clapped her hands and shouted, "Wait! I've got to get my camera! I want to get a picture of this for my website!"

He rolled his eyes. Just the sort of thing he should have expected.

But Uncle Jake nodded approvingly and shooed her on toward the house. "Yes sirree, gotta save this day for posterity. One day your grandkids'll be looking at it and you can say, 'This is where it all started.'"

In the hubbub of greetings, Brandon whispered to his uncle, "What are you up to?"

"Up to?" Uncle Jake inspected the head of his hammer. "What makes you think I'm up to anything? *Maybe* I'm just here to make sure *you* aren't up to anything. Don't sell your soul, Brandon. Nothing's worth that. If you're doing this for the wrong reasons, you just pack up and go on home to that dinky apartment of yours."

Brandon forced himself not to squirm as he looked his uncle in the eye and lied. "You said it yourself, Uncle Jake. It was nobody's fault but ours that we couldn't produce that receipt. I'm just being neighborly."

"Same here, same here."

"But, are you, um, sure you're up to it?"

"Course I'm up to it. Fit as a fiddle. That doctor doesn't know what he's talking about, telling me to watch out for my ol' ticker. What's those pills he gives me for if they don't fix me up?"

Becca and Mee-Maw came bearing big covered casserole dishes, with Ryan trailing behind, a mountain of something covered in tinfoil in his hands.

"What is all this?" Brandon asked as he jogged ahead of the women to get the door.

"Thank you kindly, Brandon," Mee-Maw said as she negotiated the porch steps—new from the look of them, to match the equally new back stoop added on in the week or so since Brandon had agreed to arrange the construction of the pole barn. "Phew, when is it gonna get any cooler?" Mee-Maw asked. "This is just a little something to tide us over, so you menfolk won't have to stop for dinner."

"A little something? Mee-Maw, that—"

He was interrupted by Penelope, who'd stepped to the back door with her camera. "Oh! For me? A housewarming?"

"A barn raisin'. This here is some squash I put up this summer, and Becca there has some butter beans. Ryan's got the ham I baked last night after it cooled off."

"Come in, come in!" Penelope moved aside to allow the women to pass by her. "Thank you so much! Kitchen's right in here. Put it in the fridge. Let me get that for you…"

Brandon exchanged a wry look with Ryan. "Did Uncle Jake rope you into this?"

"I think this was something Mee-Maw and Uncle Jake worked out." Ryan shrugged.

"Hey, I just show up where Becca and Mee-Maw tell me. Works out better that way, I've found. Besides, no way you're going to get that barn raised in a day with just kids. And it's supposed to start raining tomorrow." He moved across the threshold to be relieved of his tin-foil-covered mountain of ham.

Brandon cast a backward glance off the back porch at the sky and steadily rising sun. If they didn't get to work, they wouldn't get anything accomplished.

Ryan must have thought the same thing. "Ready?" he asked.

"Yup. Let's hit it."

Brandon loped down the porch steps, Ryan behind him, and headed toward the men knotted around the materials. "I sure appreciate you guys coming out to give us a hand."

A rumble of tires on gravel and someone's hiss of disgust made him stop. Brandon turned to see another pickup trundle up the driveway.

It was the last person he wanted to see.

Richard Murphy.

PENELOPE STOPPED in the midst of getting-to-know-you conversation with Mrs. MacIntosh—

Mee-Maw, she said to call her—and Becca. Voices loud with anger filtered through the bungalow's walls.

Mee-Maw peered with her through the window over the kitchen sink and compressed her lips. "Murphy," she muttered.

Penelope took a half step back at the old woman's vehemence. She recalled what Brandon had warned her about reaction to her grandfather. At the time she'd thought he was exaggerating.

"I'd better get out there and pull Ryan back." Becca started for the door. "No telling what he'll do. Doesn't Murphy have any better sense—"

"No. Let me." Penelope walked to the door. "I don't know what you think my grandfather has done to you. But he is my grandfather, and he's always welcome here."

Becca started to speak, but Mee-Maw held up a hand. "She's right, Becca. This is her house, and we have insulted her hospitality. Penelope, I do apologize. It's just that this is the first time I've seen him…since…" Again her eyes clouded over. "We'll get Ryan to run us on home."

"No. Why does it have to be this way?" Penelope protested. "Why is it that the man I know and love can create such a violent reaction? He's not the monster you think he is."

Mee-Maw treated her to intense scrutiny. Apparently, by the harrumphing noise she made in her throat, she was satisfied with what she saw. "Can't help who you're kin to, I reckon, but you'd best get out there. Brandon and Ryan are looking for all the world like they're gonna bodily remove him."

Penelope nodded, sucked in another lungful of air and pushed open the back door.

"…not welcome here! Why don't you go back to the posse of high-dollar defense lawyers you've got working for you and see if you can wiggle out of that federal indictment?" Brandon was saying.

"You and MacIntosh here put such store by family, well, this is my family's land. I'm welcome any ol' time I choose to come."

"Grandpa."

The crowd of onlookers switched its focus to Penelope.

"Penny-girl. You tell that boy to back off!"

She hated the skewering looks from the

men who'd come to help her almost as much as she hated the position her grandfather had put her in.

Penelope wondered how her mother might handle this situation and came up at a loss. Marlene Murphy Langston had always been closemouthed about her Georgia roots and her dad, as though she were somehow ashamed of them.

Right now, with her grandfather and Brandon standing toe-to-toe, insight would have been supremely useful.

She closed her hand over her grandfather's meaty arm and led him closer to his truck.

"Grandpa, you're, um, not the most popular guy at the party here, are you?" she said lightly.

"Maybe you're not hanging around the best quality of people, Penny. I told you to stay away from Brandon Wilkes and Ryan MacIntosh, and you got both of 'em here."

"They're helping me build a pole barn."

"I'm a trifle disappointed in you, Penny-girl. Why are you accepting charity from the likes of them? They're using you, Penny, using you to get to me."

"Grandpa Murphy, I can't build this barn on my own. And they're helping. You might as well know—I've told Brandon he can use the land in exchange for helping me with the barn."

She steeled herself for an explosion. His expression darkened and his eyes grew cold and hard.

But then her grandfather relaxed. He nodded in a thoughtful way. "You're just doing what you have to do, hmm?"

Before she could answer, he seemed to have made up his mind. "Well, I'm in the way here. You go ahead, let them help you. If it had been three months ago, I would have had a crew that could have thrown up that pole barn in a day's time. But I lost all that. I lost all of it because of those two men standing right there." He jutted his chin toward Brandon and Ryan. "So I guess it's fitting they help you. Sort of makes up for me not being able to. Just… Penny-girl, don't forget. You can't trust him. Don't get sweet on that big lug of a deputy, you hear?"

He bent and planted a big kiss on her cheek, squeezed her in a hug.

"Well, I'll be on my way, now, Penny-girl!" he said in a voice that rang out over the open field. "Let me know when they're all done, and I'll come back."

He slammed the truck door shut behind him, started the engine and backed out. In his wake, he left Penelope feeling as though she hadn't stood up for her grandfather...and Brandon glaring at her with deep suspicion.

CHAPTER NINE

AN AWKWARD SILENCE stretched out as the rumble of Grandpa Murphy's truck faded in the distance. Brandon wasn't the only suspicious one in the group.

Penelope's feet felt heavy and the optimism snuffed out inside her as she crossed the dewy ground to the men.

"That's your grandpa?" someone asked.

She nodded. "Yes. Yes, he is." She thought about all the times her mother had compressed her lips and shaken her head when the subject of Penelope's grandfather had come up. Penelope, until this moment, had always thought it was because her mom was ashamed of her South Georgia roots.

Some of the men standing in the semicircle facing her shuffled their feet and stared at the ground. One of them suddenly straightened, removed his baseball cap and wiped at his face in the early morning mugginess.

"Well, I reckon I'd better get on out of y'all's way," he said. "Just came by to wish you well on that pole barn. Got a heap of my own work to get to."

Penelope saw Brandon's and Uncle Jake's surprise and realized the man was making excuses he hadn't felt the need to make earlier.

She forced a polite smile. "Thank you so much. I appreciate you coming by this morning. It means a lot to me."

The man replaced his cap, tipped it at her and strode off to his truck. A moment of silence stretched thin, followed by another defector making the walk to his truck.

When the third man started to speak, Brandon interrupted him.

"Jarvis, I know you don't have a bit of lost love for Murphy, but you were saying not five minutes ago how you were here to help. Now, I think you should hear Penelope out at least, give her that courtesy."

Penelope caught her breath at Brandon's defense of her. Her wonderment grew when Uncle Jake spoke up.

"Out of everybody standin' here, I reckon I

got done as dirty by Richard Murphy as any of us, 'cept maybe Ryan and his grandma. Pardon me, Miss Penelope, if I don't mince my words about your kinfolk, but the truth's the truth. The rat stole my land, this land we're standin' on right here. And he did even worse to Ryan's grandma than just run her out of the house she'd lived in for sixty years or more." Uncle Jake paused, stared at Penelope.

Again, she was so shocked at the vitriol her grandfather could engender that she was rendered speechless.

Uncle Jake pushed on. "But a girl has to be loyal to her family. If she's not, well, then, she won't be loyal to anybody. Now I say—" he tapped his finger on the bib of his overalls "—this stops here. We don't take out our anger on a man's children or his children's children, not unless they're picking a fight with us. Miss Penelope, you can settle this once and for all. Why'd you come here?"

"I just wanted…dirt and a house. It seemed like a good opportunity."

"And it is," Uncle Jake declared. "Ain't no better place on earth than Brazelton County to call home. Now, time's a-wasting, and I got to go feed the hogs this evening. Brandon, what do you need me to do?"

The other men seemed mollified by Uncle Jake's pronouncement and his offer to help. As talk once again dissolved into the nuts and bolts of the job before them, a yellow school bus jounced up the driveway.

Penelope felt a touch on her arm. She glanced away from the boys now bursting off the bus and saw Brandon smiling. "We'll get it done," he promised.

TEN HOURS LATER, twilight gathering and the heat of the day cooling off, Penelope offered a tired farewell wave to Uncle Jake and Jarvis and the other farmers who'd come to help. The schoolboys had left hours ago.

Now only Brandon remained. But where was he? She glanced up at the shiny metal roof on her new barn, amazed at how much work they'd accomplished in a day's time. The pole barn had, with all the labor available, been almost a shazam-now-you-see-it feat.

Sure, the doors still weren't hung, the water supply and electricity weren't hooked up, and the inside shelves she'd planned weren't installed, but it was shelter. A place to work. A place to make her dreams come true.

She walked around the corner of the house to see Brandon, shirtless, standing at an outside spigot, water rushing into his open hands. He didn't hear her at first as he splashed the water on his face, arms and chest.

The twilight revealed his well-built body, not an ounce of spare fat anywhere. She didn't see the gym-sculpted, steroid-assisted six-pack. No, this was the real thing, the result of hours of physical labor, form beautifully following function.

An urge to sculpt such a body overtook Penelope. The urge to recreate those planes and angles with her hands.

The splashing halted abruptly as Brandon caught her staring at him. He quickly tugged his T-shirt back over his head. She pulled herself together and said, "You, um, could have come in the house. I have hot water inside, you know."

"Well, soap and hot water would be nice."

"C'mon." She indicated the house with a jerk of her head and turned to hide her scarlet face. What was the matter with her? She, who'd painted and sculpted using male models, was acting like a schoolgirl. How could this man's bare chest undo her?

Inside, Theo wound around her ankles only to jerk back from the strange feet that clomped in behind her. "It's okay, Theo. Everybody's gone now except Brandon," she reassured the Siamese, adding a scratch under his chin.

"That cat doesn't like me one whit."

"He just doesn't know you. And men make him nervous. The last man he had any dealings with was the vet who, um, did the snip-snip deal on him." Penelope straightened. "I have some of that ham Mee-Maw brought. Can I interest you in a sandwich?"

"Oh, man, could you ever." Brandon grinned. "I'm so hungry I could eat the hole out of a doughnut. But—" he looked down at himself, his T-shirt dusty and damp "—I'm not fit for the dinner table, I'm afraid."

"Neither am I. I've got some extra large T-shirts that I keep for…" She trailed off, not wanting to share how she used men's T-shirts for pajamas. "Why don't you grab a shower, and I'll get us something to eat?"

"Nope. Ladies first. You shower, and then I'll take you up on the hot water and the sandwich. I'll wait."

HEARING THE SHOWER water drum relentlessly down the hall unsettled Brandon. All he could think about was Penelope.

He prowled around the small living room for anything to distract him.

And there was plenty. Penelope had settled in and unpacked some of those boxes. Black-and-white photos of a rocky coast—maybe the Pacific—dominated one wall. Big sea lions sunning on rocks, and huge fir trees in the distance. Others captured a beach swathed in fog and mist, some with a definite but unidentifiable silhouette of a human figure in them.

The prints all bore "Langston" and a number on them. Brandon was impressed by their quality.

Other photos, these more candid and more like what he would take, graced the mantelpiece. In these, a woman with Penelope's dark hair and smile, a man who had Penelope's eyes. A younger man, slightly older than Penelope in the photos, had the cocky, self-confident look of an older brother.

In every photo, Penelope's smile looked forced, as though she was pretending to be at ease.

The one thing he didn't see was very much resemblance to Richard Murphy.

The water stopped running in the bathroom. Penelope would be out any second.

Brandon steeled himself. He could not afford to be distracted by a woman who possessed, at least temporarily, his uncle's land.

Maybe you're afraid she'll get too close and you'll lose the will to fight her for this land if it comes down to that.

Brandon shook off the thought. He could— and would—do anything it took to get this land back and see Murphy get handed the justice he deserved. But he had to keep his focus; who knew how much he could really trust Penelope? He'd seen her loyalty to Murphy.

So focus. She might be using you, the same way you're using her.

Behind him, he heard Penelope clear her throat. He turned around and completely lost all his good intentions. Her curly hair was still damp from the shower, and some sort of flowery shampoo wafted in his direction. He wanted to sweep her in his arms and kiss her senseless.

"All yours," she said, and Brandon wished it were that simple.

He did the only thing he thought would help: ran for the coldest shower imaginable. But her scent clung to the T-shirt she'd laid out for him, the towels she put out for him to use, the very steam that hung in the air.

"Get a grip!" he ordered himself as he dried off and pulled the T-shirt over his head.

In the kitchen, he found Penelope piling a mountain of ham, lettuce and tomatoes on a sandwich.

"Feel better?" she asked.

"Yeah. I do. That looks good."

"Can't take credit for it. It's all Mee-Maw. Those tomatoes are from her garden. When I was in New York, I would have killed for tomatoes like that in October."

Brandon shrugged and filched a piece of

ham off the sandwich. She swatted at his hand but missed. "Welcome to South Georgia. Sometimes, if the weather's warm, you can wind up with tomatoes at Christmas. Sometimes the first hard frost comes before Halloween. This is a warm year."

"The weather's nice, that's for sure." She finished the sandwiches and set them on the dinette table. "Now you can eat. No nibbling."

"I'd like to see some rain. It's awfully dry, and if we have another dry winter, we're going to be that much more in the hole next spring."

Her chuckle was a warm little burble. "Farmers and the weather. You're never satisfied, are you?"

"Oh, we could be. If we could get rain on a subscription service, delivered just when we need it, that'd be great."

"A plus for sculpting is that it's not usually weather-dependent."

"So, how is the sculpture? Have you been able to get any buyers?" The hope that she hadn't, that she was still desperate for money, felt unnatural to him. It wasn't like him to wish another person ill.

She tensed, and for an instant he saw the girl in the photos. Brandon put up his hands. "None of my business, I know."

Penelope dropped the sandwich on her plate. She bit her lip and didn't meet his eyes for a moment. "No, it's not that. Only I've had no luck yet. It's hard to sell an idea that's not tailored to a business. This one—*Love at Infinity*—I came up with for the home office of an online dating firm. That's how it works. A corporation decides it needs some culture, I do some interviews with the big dogs, and then I come up with an idea that will sum up their mission or corporate message."

"But you're trying. It will happen." Now Brandon did feel like a heel, hoping for the exact opposite. Why couldn't she just pick up and move somewhere else so he could sincerely root for her?

"I'm getting hits on my website every day. So sure, yeah, it will happen."

Was she trying to convince him or herself? Brandon had to admit she wasn't hugely successful either way.

"So what if someone wanted you to do something different? Would you?"

"Sure. Of course. I'd put this one on the back burner."

They ate in silence for a few moments before Brandon switched the subject. "Those pictures in the living room? You took them? They're good."

"Yeah. That's Oregon, near where Lewis and Clark saw the Pacific Ocean for the first time. I'd like to pretend that's how they saw it."

"It must be strange, to be so far from home."

She considered his comment and then shook her head. "No. I've never felt like I belonged anywhere. My brother, Trent, now he's the family's pride and joy."

Penelope's voice was absent of any malice or envy, just bemusement. She added, "They always want to know, 'Why can't you be more like your brother?' He's the one who followed them into real estate. I grew up in Portland, but about ten years ago, my parents moved to Bend—you probably never heard of it."

"So you're the artsy one?"

She sighed. "Yeah. Definitely marching to the beat of a different drummer, that's me. I'm twenty-eight, but my parents still treat me as though I'm their baby. My mom kept saying this commission was too good to be true." She grimaced. "What about you? Brothers? Sisters?"

"One kid brother." Brandon didn't feel like volunteering the story of his life. Come to think of it, he'd never had to tell any girl that he'd dated much about himself. They'd known. Life in a small town meant never having to talk about painful things if you didn't want to, because people already knew your secrets. So if Penelope wanted to know more, she could ask her dear old granddad.

But she didn't let up. "So how about your parents? Do your mom and dad still live around here?"

"Uh, no." The referral to his long-absent father stung. Had Murphy already filled her in on Brandon's dad deserting his mom with two little kids? He got up and took his plate to the sink. "My mom passed away a couple of years ago. Say, why'd your mom move so far away? I mean, she was from Georgia, right?"

A long silence told him that Penelope wanted to talk about that about as much as he wanted to talk about his family. "My dad was from there. My mom moved away from Georgia when my grandmother divorced Grandpa Murphy. Mom and Dad met in college and moved back to Oregon to be near his family."

"So you were never around your grandfather that much? In Georgia, I mean."

"No, not much. My mom and Grandpa Murphy never got along that well, especially after my grandmother divorced him."

Score one for the mom's smarts. Behind him, he heard Penelope's chair scrape on the floor as she pushed it back. Still, he jumped when she brushed against him as she joined him at the sink.

"I want to thank you," she said. "For today. You and your uncle both. I know you don't have much use for my grandfather. But, Brandon, he's not…he's not like you think he is."

She stopped short, shook her head. Brandon looked at her to see a droplet of water

inch down her throat from one of the ringlets
of her hair. He ached to reach over and cap-
ture it with a fingertip. But he'd be touching
Richard Murphy's granddaughter, and he just
couldn't do that.

"Anyway. What I was saying." Her voice
was husky. "I think it's great that you guys
rose above your dislike of my grandfather and
helped me out. The barn is wonderful, but
more than that, the feeling of community was
terrific. I can't put it into words. And what
your uncle said, about all this hate stopping
here? He changed those men's minds, Brandon, and he didn't have to do that. I really
appreciate it."

Brandon clutched the plate tighter and
scrubbed the already clean surface. She was
so close that the scent of her hair or her body
lotion or something that smelled incredibly
good beat out the lemon scent of the dish de-
tergent.

He started to speak, to force out something
meaningless, maybe, *it was nothing* or *my
pleasure*.

But then, without warning, she rose up on

tiptoe and brushed her lips against his cheek. "Thank you," she whispered. "Thank you." And then she bolted out the screen door.

CHAPTER TEN

A RATTLE AGAINST the window's miniblinds shook Penelope loose from her last remnants of sleep. She rolled over and groaned. Opening one eye, she confirmed that Theo was on her vanity table, pawing at the blinds.

"Theo. Just this once, can you please, please, use the litter box? It's clean. At least, I think it's clean. Yeah. It's clean. If you go out, I have to go and watch you. And I don't care what time it is. It's too early. I got no sleep last night."

Theo cast a baleful look her way and made a flying leap onto Penelope's stomach. She grunted under the weight of his not-so-gentle landing. Obviously, the litter box plea was not working.

And neither was Penelope's attempt to forget her idiocy the previous night. She'd kissed him. She'd kissed Brandon Wilkes.

Okay, not a full-on mouth kiss, but a kiss. On the cheek, her lips against his jaw.

And man if it hadn't felt good. The memory of his five-o'clock shadow scraping against her lips, the fresh scent of him...

"Aaargh!" Theo jumped back.

Penelope reached up and gave him a reassuring pet. "Not you. I'm not mad at you. I'm mad at me."

And she was. Somehow she'd managed to get caught up in her emotions and kiss the man who'd called her grandfather a what?

A thief and an extortionist.

She scrunched her fingers through her hair. Maybe if she pulled hard enough, she'd yank some brain cells loose.

At least he'd had the decency to be gone when she'd returned to the house. Of course, she had paced behind her new barn—the barn that he'd built—long enough for him to get the message.

She'd come back to find a note.

Thanks for supper. Glad you like the barn. Will be back to see it when you have it all finished.

He'd signed it with a scrawled BAW, leaving her choosing and discarding all the possible middle names he could have.

She'd kissed him.

Theo yowled, then reached over and gave her a nip on the hand she had clenched in the covers.

"Ow! Cut that out. Why is it that Siamese think nipping is the way to—oh, why am I arguing with a cat? Come on. I'll let you out."

She pushed Theo to one side and tossed the covers back. He wrapped himself in ecstatic figure eights around her ankles as she made her way to the back door.

"Yes, yes, this is what all men like to do, pester you till they get their way—"

She was interrupted by the *Ride of The Valkyries*. Literally.

Mom. On her cell phone.

"Sorry, Theo. I dare not let it go to voice mail. Hold on. I'll be back."

A dash and a bellyflop across her unmade bed netted her the phone before it made that ominous missed-call beep. "Mom? What time is it out there?"

Penelope squinted at the clock, but the

glare from the now-open miniblinds obscured the numbers.

"Six-thirty. I'm up to do my yoga. You didn't return my calls yesterday."

"I was busy?" The attempt at a reply sounded lame even to her.

Her mother tsked. "I called you three times yesterday. And you were so busy you couldn't pick up the phone or call me *once?*"

"I was. Mom. Honest. I was building a barn."

Her mother paused while she processed that information. "All by yourself?"

"Well, no. Some neighbors were helping. But we didn't finish until late and then I had dinner and…" Penelope thought about just who she'd had dinner with, and the kiss that followed it, and she couldn't suppress a whimper. From what? Humiliation? Shame? Hunger for more kisses?

"What is it? I know that sound. That's your I-can't-believe-I-did-that groan. Spill it."

"Mom. Believe it or not, there are some things in my life I do not wish to spill to you. No offense."

"None taken. Well, not much. But I worry,

Penelope. You're out there, all by yourself, alone in the middle of nowhere."

Penelope tried to interrupt the tidal wave of doubts, worries and maternal neuroses that was coming, but she'd waited too late to stop the onslaught. In the midst of the why-can't-you-get-a-normal-job-and-live-in-a-normal-place-for-once-in-your-life speech, Theo stalked back in and took another nip on her toe.

"Ow! Theo, honestly! Mom, I've got to let the cat out."

"I thought that's what litter boxes were for."

"He's picky and you know it."

"Well, don't hang up. I'll never get you back on the phone, so don't let the cat be an excuse for you to say, 'Mom, I'm really, terrifically busy and I've got to go now.' How busy can you be?"

Penelope stumbled out the bedroom door, trying her best not to trip on the cat as she headed down the hall and toward the kitchen. "Busy. Really, really busy."

"No. You can't be busy. Because your grandfather called yesterday, completely out of the blue, and told me that you don't have a sale for your sculpture. Is this true?"

"Mom!" Penelope braced herself against the kitchen door. Theo stopped midstride, looked back over his shoulder and sat down in a huff.

He could just wait. Right now, more than anything, Penelope wanted to bang her head against the wall. How could Grandpa Murphy do this to her? How could he?

"I take that to be a yes? Penelope, why didn't you call us immediately? But no, I had to hear such news from my father, when you *know* I don't like talking with the man. You need our help, Penelope. You have that loan, you're going to be in default, your credit will never recover."

"Listen, please. I have a plan, okay? I have time. I don't need rescuing."

"Obviously you do or else you wouldn't have taken leave of your senses. Your grandfather wants you to sell the place to a solid-waste dump! Are you seriously considering that? You can't. Think what it would do to the environment."

Theo was back to weaving figure eights

around Penelope's ankles, only this time also yowling passionately.

"What is that sound? What are you doing to that cat?"

"I told you. I'm trying to let the cat out. Only, I can't because I just woke up but I'm not awake and I'm trying to tell you that I haven't sold—oh, let me let the cat out."

Penelope marched over to the door. She threw it open to see Brandon on the back steps.

She gasped. For a full second, all she could think about was the fact that she was wearing nothing but a camisole and a pair of tiny sleep shorts she'd gotten on sale at Victoria's Secret. Then her reflexes mercifully kicked in and she was able to slam the door shut. A nanosecond too late, she realized Theo was now on *Brandon's* side of the door.

"Penelope? Penelope?"

She heard her mother's screech through the phone. "I swear, Penelope, if you don't answer me, I'm calling nine-one-one!"

"Mom, I'm okay, no, I'll never be okay again. I just flashed the next door neighbor."

"Is that all?" Her mother huffed. "I thought someone had broken in on you."

"No. Oh, how do I ever face him again? Mom, I kissed him last—" Penelope stuffed her fingers into her mouth and bit down hard.

"Mmm. You did?"

Penelope pulled her fingers back out of her mouth. "Not now. I have to figure out how to get the cat back in without facing Brandon."

"Brandon Wilkes?"

"Yes." Some of her humiliation faded. "How did you—"

"Your grandfather doesn't think too much of him. He says he's a bad influence."

"Oh, well, Mom, it's complicated."

"But then, your grandfather is not the most credible judge of character." This last was delivered with a crisp edge. "In fact, that's one reason I worry so much about you. Down there. With your grandfather. Who's probably yanking your chain like nobody's business."

Penelope winced. "Listen, I'd love to continue this conversation. But I have a man who I just flashed on my porch, my cat's outside, and I'm wearing next to nothing. Can I please, please, please call you back later?"

"If you *will* call me back later. But will you?"

"I swear. Solemnly. By the light of the moon. By my firstborn child. By…sheesh, Mom. I've gotta go. Love you!"

"I'll be waiting. Love you." Her mother hung up.

Now. Brandon. Penelope put a palm to her forehead. "Are you still there?" she called out.

"Yep. Still here. Is the cat supposed to be out?"

"He goes out. First thing in the morning. But watch him, okay? Or he'll wander off."

"So should I bring him back in? You decent?"

"Not so much. Hold on." Penelope made another mad dash. She flung open drawers until she laid her hands on a pair of jeans and shimmied into them. With lightning-fast fingers, she finished dressing, ran a brush through her hair and then stopped. She had to get hold of herself.

Penelope closed her eyes and drew in a deep breath of air. In through the nose, out through the mouth, like her yoga instructor had taught her. Center. Calm. Peace.

The traitorous peace left her, though, as soon as she opened her eyes again.

No two ways about it. She had to face Brandon.

BRANDON LEANED against the porch post, tried to keep an eye on that cat, and failed miserably to erase the image of Penelope from his brain.

Man, but she was beautiful.

Focus. Focus.

He pinched himself on the thigh. This woman would drive him crazy if he let her. He hadn't gotten any sleep the night before, feeling by turn guilty that he was actively planning to take advantage of her financial situation and hating that she couldn't see what a crook her grandfather was so that he could feel free to…

What? Sweep her off her feet?

The cat cast a glance over his shoulder. Then he took off running for the open field. Brandon leaped off his perch and made a grab for him. Yowling and hissing, the cat communicated loud and clear that he didn't appreciate being manhandled.

Now what to do? Brandon eyed the cat, who struggled in his hold. "Oh, no, you don't, buster. And don't you even think about scratching me. I have orders, and they are not to let you wander off."

Hoping he'd made his point, Brandon put the cat down on the porch. The cat whirled around and hiked his tail up toward Brandon. It was as if he were saying, *If I were a skunk, you'd be sprayed now, buddy.*

The cat sat down and regarded him with blue eyes narrowed to slits.

"You don't care much for me, do you?" Brandon toed the new lumber that had been used for the back steps. "Well, truth be told, I am more of a dog person. But I usually get along with cats. So, what is it?"

The cat swished its tail like a whip.

"Oh. You're like Uncle Jake. You think I'm up to no good, huh?" His stomach roiled, and he couldn't be sure whether it was the hard-as-a-brick biscuit Uncle Jake had cooked that morning or Brandon's uneasy conscience.

"Hey, it's not like I'm the one who lost her sculpture sale for her," Brandon muttered.

The cat flattened its ears as if it knew what

he was plotting. "If you don't like me, you'd really hate Murphy. He won't have an animal on his place that he can't eat."

He took in the shape of the barn against the horizon. What he'd said yesterday, in her defense, had felt heavy on his tongue. He'd seen the confused looks the other guys had given him. But how could he explain, *Hey, look, guys, this is for me, really. You're not helping her. I'm just letting her subsidize the materials, and I'm going to pick up the whole thing for a song.* He couldn't.

And then Uncle Jake had said his piece, and Brandon had felt even more of a jerk. But...this was their land. He should be breaking it up for winter wheat, not standing on the porch steps of a totally unnecessary house that took up the most fertile part of the tract. All because some woman wanted her "dirt and a house."

She could have had her dirt anywhere. Why did she have to have this dirt? His dirt?

The back door swung open. Brandon looked up and saw Penelope, this time fully clothed. Part of him was disappointed at the cover-up, but the saner part of him was glad of it. If he wanted to get her off this land, then he didn't need any part of him wanting her to stay.

CHAPTER ELEVEN

"Ahem." Penelope plastered a big smile on her face and looked at Brandon. Theo streaked back inside as if Brandon was the type to tie a bottle rocket to his tail.

Hmm. If Theo doesn't trust him...

"Well. I see you are decent, after all."

Penelope felt her smile falter. He could have been gentleman enough to ignore her faux pas. Undeterred, she forced the corners of her mouth back up.

"Yes. Yes, I am. Can I interest you in some coffee? I just put a pot on."

Brandon gazed off across the field and up into the sky, as though he was gauging the time of day by the position of the sun. "Kind of late for your first pot of coffee, isn't it? Or is that how you artists do things?"

She folded her arms against her chest. "Don't you *ever* go to work as a deputy?"

"I do. At night. In the morning when I get

off, I farm. Or at least I try to farm. You, on the other hand, obviously sleep in."

She ground her teeth at his snarkiness... "I never claimed to be a morning person."

"You'd never make it in farming then, would you?"

"Just what *is* your problem?" she couldn't help snapping. "I was bothering no one, and I open my back door to let my cat out and there *you* are, lurking around my back steps. And now you—you—"

"That how you always let the cat out? I think it's only fair to warn you—even though you are in the country, word will get around. Your place might become a popular destination."

Penelope opened her mouth to speak, then shut her lips tight. A moment later, she managed a much more subdued, "Are you always this grouchy this early? Or is it just me who has this effect on you?"

His eyebrows shot up. She'd found her mark, or maybe hit too close to home.

"I see." Penelope clasped her arms tighter around herself. "I do apologize for upsetting your equilibrium."

Brandon's eyes flashed. "You do *not* have any sort of effect on me. None. I'm...the day is wasting, that's all. I have to go in at lunch today, and I've spent more time than I care babysitting that cat of yours. The thing doesn't like me."

"An instinct I trust implicitly, thank you very much."

Brandon threw up his hands. "Look, let's start fresh. Good morning or day or whatever it is at nearly ten. I wanted to tell you that I would be working in the field back here. That's all."

Oh. What had she expected? Him to say, *Didn't sleep a wink, either, and came here so I can give you a proper kiss?*

I need my head examined.

"Okay. You want to work. I have no problem with it."

"Well, then, you wouldn't mind moving your car, now would you?"

"My car? It's in the front and you want—"

"Because it's in the driveway. Blocking my path. The county dragged such a deep ditch alongside the road, I can't get the tractor through here except up your driveway.

Which was stupid of the county because before you moved in, I could have accessed it at any point." He closed his eyes, and she could tell he was trying to contain himself.

"Oh." She couldn't think of anything else to say. "Let me get my keys."

A few minutes later, she parked her car out of the tractor's path. It was a big, old thing, dented and gouged with streaks of rust. Unlike her Grandpa Murphy's tractors, sold off at auction to pay off the notes on them, Brandon's didn't have a climate-controlled enclosed cab, which meant no CD player. No plush upholstered seat. The one accommodation to the operator's comfort was a car radio attached with ratty blue wires to the steering wheel's column and a rigged-up box of speakers behind the metal seat.

"What now?" Brandon snapped over the thrum of the engine.

"Nothing. I was—your tractor is—older than I would have expected."

"It's older than I am, but it still works. Unlike some people, I don't borrow to the hilt for flashy equipment."

The comment stung. Sure, her grandfather

had borrowed operating capital, but you had to spend money to make money. If you didn't invest back…

But before she could even finish the thought, he'd started pulling away.

"Wait!"

Brandon worked his jaw and stopped the tractor from its slow roll. "Yes?"

Penelope had no idea where the next words came from. "I've never been on a tractor. Can you give me a ride?"

She was sure, from his expression, that he was going to bang his head against the steering wheel.

"Now?"

She grinned. "Uh, no time like the present?"

She saw composure settle his expression like a curtain dropping at the end of a show.

Somehow Penelope liked the barely contained anger better than his carefully schooled expression.

"Sure," Brandon replied. "No time like the present. But it will have to be a quick one, because I really do need to get some ground broken."

He hopped off the tractor. With impersonal hands, he assisted her as she got up. She felt the seat warm from his body heat as she dropped into it.

"Okay. Just put it in gear and go," he said, jumping to the ground.

Penelope yanked her hands from the wheel as if it was on fire. "No! That wasn't—I mean, I can't drive a tractor!"

"Why not? I learned how to drive one before I could drive a car." Now she saw his thinly disguised amusement.

"Well, I don't want to break it. Or tear it up. Or something. I thought you'd drive it."

To her relief, his composure started fraying at the edges. Yes. That was better. Not so condescending.

He put his hands on his hips and surveyed her. "I had no idea you'd go all girly on me. You weld. And build stuff."

"But I can't drive a tractor. At least," she said, and smiled again, "not until you show me how."

He pursed his lips, the same lips Penelope had fantasized about way too much the night before.

He shook his head and swung up beside her.

"Scootch up. This seat's not big enough for us to sit beside each other."

With his legs wrapped around her, she found herself leaning against the rock-solid chest she'd admired the evening before. His arms came around her middle and he took hold of the steering wheel just above where her own hands had settled.

Her pulse rate ratcheted up with each successive point of physical contact between them. Penelope gripped the wheel.

This was playing with fire.

The tractor jerked forward and Brandon leaned down to her ear. "Hold on! It's going to be a bumpy ride!"

BRANDON WAS going out of his mind.

He breathed in a gasp of diesel-infused exhaust to counteract the floral smell that wafted up from her hair. Insane. He was insane. She was purposefully driving him nuts so that he couldn't—

Wait a minute. She didn't know, did she? She didn't have any idea that he was trying to encroach on her—his—land. Or did she?

Maybe she had her own agenda. Maybe she and Murphy together had some plot hatched that would put his to shame.

And then she laughed, that rich bubbly laugh that, in combination with all the physical contact, nearly sent him over the edge.

"This is fun!" Penelope shrieked. He took in her flushed cheeks, warm brown eyes, parted lips that absolutely begged to be kissed. No artifice there, or if there was, she was such a good actress that he couldn't tell.

"So which knob do I pull to put the, er, thingamabob down?" she asked.

Brandon dragged his brain out of the gutter and guided her hand to the proper lever. She cried out in surprise as the tractor jerked when the turning plow dropped into the soil. He put a reflexive hand on her waist to steady her.

"Easy," he told her. "Now, we go a little slower, especially in this hard ground, or else the tractor can buck up."

Brandon couldn't help but appreciate the way Penelope seemed to soak up everything he said, listen intently to his instructions.

"You're sure you've never operated a tractor before?" he asked as they got up to speed.

Penelope looked back over her shoulder. "My first time ever, but it's fun! I can see why you like it."

"Yeah, right, see how fun it is after you've been bounced around from sunup to sundown." But he said it without conviction. He couldn't fathom anybody wanting to do anything else. The air was cool against his arms, the tractor felt sure and steady under his hands. And he was plowing land he hadn't turned in more than two years. With a pretty girl along for the ride, to boot.

He grinned down at her. Why not? Enjoy the moment. Enjoy the ride.

But looming on the horizon ahead of them was Murphy's fence.

CHAPTER TWELVE

THE SUN GLITTERED off the dewdrops caught in spiderwebs along the wire fence. The sight of it carried Brandon back to the morning he'd first seen that fence carving up his uncle's land.

It had been ugly then. It was still ugly now.

"Hey, what's wrong? What did I do wrong?" Penelope asked.

Brandon couldn't even frame his thoughts to put them into words. He popped the clutch on the tractor and slowed his approach.

"Oh! The fence, I get it."

Did she? Brandon didn't think so. She couldn't possibly understand how that boundary line rankled him. It was all he could do not to floor the accelerator and plow through it.

It wasn't just that it was a reminder of what Murphy had taken. In real, concrete ways, it meant that he'd lost even more land to Murphy, because he had to figure in the turn-around space for the tractor. At least, though, no trees or brush grew up along it. He'd made sure he'd sprayed it these past three years with herbicide to keep it clean.

Because one day that fence was coming down.

"So we just turn around? And plow back across the field?" Penelope was asking.

"Yeah, that's about it."

What did she expect of him, anyway? She'd imposed herself on him this morning.

Be honest, bud. You were enjoying it yourself. You could have said no.

He hated that. This woman was fast becoming a weakness for him.

"I'm taking you back, because I need to get some work done." This time, Brandon didn't wait around to be bamboozled. He lifted the plows, pointed the tractor down alongside the fence and headed back toward her house and the barn.

When he pulled to a stop near the barn, he switched off the engine. "So there you are, back where you belong," Brandon said after he'd helped her down.

Penelope didn't look convinced. "Right. What will you plant out there?"

"You're interested?" He paused after he'd swung one leg back over the tractor seat.

"Of course."

Was she trying some Scheherazade technique, stalling him in his effort to get this land prepped for planting? Brandon discarded the notion as plain and simple paranoia.

"Since you asked, strawberries."

Penelope blinked. He had no clue what she'd expected him to say, but obviously, it hadn't been that.

"Strawberries?"

"Yeah." He put his hand to the ignition, but her puzzlement kept him from firing up the engine.

"But you don't have any packing sheds." She frowned. "Do they even grow here in the winter?"

"You can plant them until mid-October, which means I'll have to get my butt in gear. I won't be packing and shipping them. It would be a pick-your-own kind of deal."

"Twenty-five acres of pick-your-own strawberries? You guys must really like them."

Brandon shook his head again. "I'll only plant part of it in strawberries, just enough to test out the idea. The rest I'll plant in winter wheat."

"Wait a minute. You're going to plant a pick-your-own-strawberry patch back here? But how will people access it?" Comprehension dawned in her face. "Oh, no. No, no, no. You are not going to have people trekking by my house with their buckets and baskets, asking me how to get strawberry stains out of T-shirts. No way. How on earth can I work with—"

"Hey. Harvest time isn't until spring. By then…" Brandon shrugged his shoulders. "Anything can happen." He fired up the engine and let the tractor gently chug past her.

By then, maybe you'll be long gone.

That's what he wanted, right? So why didn't the idea appeal to him as much as it used to?

PENELOPE STOMPED back up the porch steps and walked in the back door. Of all the presumptuous, arrogant—

"Hey, Penny-girl."

She froze. Grandpa Murphy sat, a newspaper spread out on her dinette table, cup of coffee in hand.

Penelope put a hand to her chest. "You gave me a heart attack, Grandpa! How'd you—"

"Well, down here, we just help ourselves. Door was unlocked. Didn't think you'd mind. Good coffee, by the way."

"Thanks," she replied uncertainly. She closed the door behind her and made her way to the cupboard for a mug.

"I see that Brandon Wilkes is on the property. Where were you? Telling him to get off?"

"Uh, yes." Somehow she didn't feel like getting into it with him over Brandon, not after the unsettling morning she'd just had.

"That barn sure does look good."

"Yes, it does, doesn't it." Penelope pulled out the chair across from Grandpa and sank into it. She hadn't eaten breakfast, maybe that's why her knees were so wobbly. She plucked a banana from the bowl of fruit in the center of the table,

Grandpa Murphy glanced up over the paper. "What's got you all shaken up?"

"Hmm." She concentrated on peeling the banana. "Mom called this morning."

Grandpa winced. "That's the way to start off a morning, Marlene chewing on your ear."

She didn't feel her usual sense of solidarity, me-and-you-against-your-mother. She blew out a breath. "Grandpa. Why did you tell Mom I'd lost my commission?"

"Ah, no. I told her to keep that to herself. Can't any woman keep her trap shut?"

Penelope tried hard not to be offended at his sexist remark. After all, he'd grown up in a different world. "That she told me is not the point. The point is you shared something I would have rather told her about on my own."

"Penny-girl…I was just worried about you. I mean, look at me, broke, in legal trouble, not even able to help you build a simple pole barn. I shouldn't have said anything. Next time I won't."

"So why did you? Why did you even call Mom? I didn't think you guys talked all that much."

"We don't. Every time we do, she manages to get my dander up, telling what everything I've done wrong, getting on that self-righteous holier-than-thou pedestal of hers. Says my troubles are my own doing. Ha! But you know, I got worried, thought about you." He flicked through the paper. "I figured she already knew about it. Didn't know I was spilling any beans. You didn't tell me to keep it from her."

"I didn't think I had to tell you. You of all people know how Mom can be."

"Oh, yeah, I know your mother. Nag, nag, nag. Just like *her* mother. Don't know how I stood that woman—"

"And now Mom's hot under the collar." Penelope knew better than to let him get going about her grandmother. "Thinks I'm going to sell to these solid-waste people."

That got his attention. He laid the paper down and stared at her. "But you are. Aren't you?"

"Grandpa, I said I would consider meeting with them. How did you hear that and think I was considering *selling* to them?"

He worked his jaw. "But, Penny-girl, you don't want to miss this opportunity. I worked for three years trying to convince these guys that this was—"

"Three years? Grandpa, you've only had this land for, what, two years?"

She couldn't read his expression, but he wagged a finger in her direction. "Now listen, young lady. Don't go distracting me. You'll be making a big mistake if you let this offer slip through your fingers. These people are serious, and they're willing to put their money where their mouth is."

With that, Grandpa shoved his chair back and jerked to his feet. "I can tell when my company's not welcome. I thought it was everybody here yesterday, and you not wanting to scare them off when they were volunteering labor. But now I'm seeing a different picture."

"No, Grandpa. Don't get all mad like this." She stood up as well. "Of course you're welcome here. And I'm sorry if yesterday hurt your feelings. I didn't mean to make you feel unwanted."

"Well, you did." His bottom lip quivered ever so slightly before he set his jaw. "I couldn't decide whether it was your mother telling you more of that hogwash about me leaving your grandmother. She left me,

Penny-girl, she left *me*." Agitated, he ran a hand through his hair.

"I know, I know," she soothed. "You've told me. And no, Mom isn't the reason. There was no—look, I'm sorry. Okay?"

"I thought we had a chance to catch up on all the time we missed. Your mama dragged you off to Oregon, and I never got to see you or that brother of yours. And here you are, old enough to make up your own mind about me, and I figured we could do this deal together, and it would be you and me."

Grandpa's eyes misted over. Penelope touched his shoulder. "Grandpa, don't do this to yourself. I am here. And of course I want you around. I'm just—I haven't said no to talking with these landfill people."

"It's not a landfill. It's solid waste. Recycling, Penny-girl. Recycling. And it would help the both of us out, you and me. You could lend me some of the money you'd get so I could pay those blood-sucking lawyers. And don't you want to stay here? You can't if you don't make a go of your sculpting. You don't want to fail with that, now do you?"

Penelope closed her eyes. "No, Grandpa. You know I don't."

"Well, then. Okay, okay, so you're not that fired up about it. I'll back off. You don't know these guys like I do. But when you meet 'em, you'll like 'em." He winked. "Trust me. You do trust me, don't you?"

She glanced past him out the window and saw Brandon's tractor as it plowed across her field. Remembered his hand on hers as he guided her to the right lever. Could she really sell the land out from under a man who loved it so much?

"Hey, I'm not hearing that you trust me," Grandpa Murphy said.

She took in his eager face, thought about the financial jam he was in. Next to his, her financial picture looked positively rosy.

How could she say no to him when he had a slam-dunk way to get the money he needed? How could she turn down any opportunity to keep him from behind bars?

Penelope managed a weak smile. "I trust you, Grandpa. Just let me have some time to get used to this land-selling idea, okay?"

CHAPTER THIRTEEN

THE CHUG of a tractor wormed its way into Penelope's consciousness as she read back over her latest proposal. Brandon started, blast him, at five o'clock in the morning, every day, and she didn't get any peace and quiet until nearly noon.

Irritated, she clicked Save on her laptop and stood to look out the kitchen window. There he was, closer than ever, a dusty wake billowing up behind his plows.

Her backyard. And he wanted to have droves of strawberry pickers back there. How was she supposed to concentrate on her sculpture if she had that much noise and people plodding around, looking at her while she worked?

Face it. You've had no bites on any of these proposals. The smart thing to do would not be tying up such expensive materials and your time into a project you can't find a buyer for.

That didn't mean she had slowed her spending of the borrowed money in her account. Since the barn had been completed, the balance had dropped considerably. Materials, the electrician's costs, the plumber's costs and the shelves she'd rigged.

But she now had a working studio, something that comforted her if she could put out of her mind how much pricey equipment she had in there.

It was hard to do that when she only had her own worried thoughts—and those of her grandpa and her mom—for company. During the past week, the only thing she'd heard from Brandon was the aggravating noise of the tractor waking her up entirely too early.

He hasn't called you. He hasn't even knocked on your back door on his way to the field.

She'd thought of a hundred different reasons to call him. *Know any cheaper electricians?* or *My welder needs shoving over a little. Can you help?* But as the phone refused to ring, all her reasons dwindled to mere excuses, and transparent ones at that.

So Penelope had shoved the welder over

herself and looked in the yellow pages for electricians. It was just as well. She could not for the life of her figure out why she couldn't get a handle on this attraction she felt for a man who despised her grandfather.

The tractor had stopped, Penelope saw, and Brandon was on the ground beside it. Kicking it? Yes, he was repeatedly kicking the back tire.

She exchanged a look with Theo, curled up on one of the dinette chairs. "Well, he's certainly not cool and calm today. Think I'll go check it out."

As she closed the distance between the house and Brandon's tractor, the uneven ground reminded her that she still had a lot of work to do to transform this place from a field to a lawn. She'd started. The petunias she'd planted along the edge of the back porch definitely cheered the place up. But she wouldn't be at a loss to fill her time.

The closer she got to Brandon, the more clearly she could hear him berating the tractor.

"Good morning." Penelope stopped just

short of the edge of the raw earth he'd churned up.

Brandon whirled around. "How long have you been standing here?"

She thought about keeping him squirming, payback for his smarmy words about her inadvertent flashing the week before. "Just walked up. I saw that you were having trouble with the tractor."

"Yeah." He glowered at it. "The third link stripped out."

"And this is bad?"

"Yeah."

"Because?" she prompted when he didn't offer anything further.

"When the eye on the third link strips out, I can't lift the plows. I could buy another one, *if* there was another in stock, but I called, and they won't have another one that will work with my hunk of junk for a week. A week!"

"Stripped out? Can you show me?"

He looked more inclined to snap her head off. "Do you happen to have a chain?"

"A chain?"

"Yeah. I've got to get this set of plows out of the field and to the welding shop in town to get it fixed. If I hurry, I can still get back in time to catch me a nap before I have to clock in at the sheriff's department at three."

She crossed over to stand next to the plows and started analyzing the way they interacted with the tractor. Penelope put a hand out and touched a long cylinder of paint-chipped cast iron with two steel eyes at each end. "Is this the third link?"

"I don't have time. Did you not hear what I was saying? I need to get this out of the field. Fine, I'll go to Uncle Jake's and get my own chain." He started toward the fence that separated her land from his uncle's.

"Wait! Cool your jets for two seconds, and let me think—"

"About what? There's nothing for you to think about!" he hollered over his shoulder.

"I might be able to fix this."

Brandon stopped in his tracks.

"I said, I might be able to—"

Brandon turned around to face her. "I heard you. But you don't know a thing about tractors."

"I know about welding. And how things work. And just because I don't know much about farming doesn't mean I'm a complete idiot. If you tell me what you need me to do, I'll bet I can use my tiny brain to figure it out."

Something in his posture relaxed. He started taking slow, halting steps toward her. "You really think…"

Penelope shrugged. "Worth a try. Unless you want to wait that week." She gestured toward her shop. "Have welder, will weld."

For the first time since she'd seen him that morning, a smile broke out on his face. "You'd do that for me?"

"Yeah. Is that such a surprise?"

He dropped his gaze to the toes of his dusty boots for a moment before meeting hers again. "Well, yeah. I'm not used to a helping hand from a Murphy."

"I'm a Langston, and furthermore, a decent human being. Yes, my grandfather is Richard Murphy, and I wish you'd get over that. You think my grandfather would turn his back on you in this situation?"

Brandon scoffed. "Oh, yeah. He's done worse."

"Look, do you want my help or not? I'm beginning to regret I offered it."

She heard him exhale sharply. "Okay. I'm sorry. Yes, if you can fix this, it would save me a lot of aggravation. I just need you to patch it for now."

Penelope leaned back over the plows, careful not to bang her ankles on the sharp points. She assessed how the eye and the sleeve went together, tried to estimate the time it would take her. "This is cast iron, right?"

"The sleeve is—the part that holds the eyes in. The eyes themselves are steel."

"That's what I thought." She straightened back up to find him standing beside her. "Well, it will take me an hour or so to weld it, and then I'll have to put blankets on it and let it cool. Cast iron can be tricky, and you don't need to rush it. I won't have this done in time for you today, but it will be ready first thing in the morning."

"You'd be saving me a week, because the shop in town would take at least that long to do the same thing. That's why I was trying to buy a new part." Brandon smiled slowly, his eyebrows knit together. "I can't believe you're doing this."

"Hey. We're neighbors. You helped me with a barn. The least I can do is weld your plow."

He chewed on his lip. "I'll pay you."

"No. No. You've done a lot for me, Brandon. Consider it my pleasure. And hey, if the welding shop guy is that backed up, maybe you'll advertise my services. That might keep the wolf from the door."

Brandon got that conflicted look on his face again, but all he said was, "Yeah. Sure. I'll be glad to do that. Good to keep the wolf from the door, right? Let me go get that chain."

WHY SHOULD HE TRUST a Murphy?

Okay, so she was, as she pointed out, a Langston, but she was still also a Murphy. And he didn't trust a Murphy as far as he could throw the moon.

Brandon jerked open the toolshed door. A storm of dust motes swirled in the ray of sunshine piercing the dim interior of the shed. He reached up for the string that operated the light, only to see, as he yanked it, the telltale flash of light signaling a blown bulb.

Great. Just great. This day was fabulous already. In the darkness, he fumbled for the chain on its hook on the wall and rustled through drawers and chests to get the tools he needed.

"Brandon? That you? 'Cause if it isn't, I got a big ol' sledgehammer in my hand and the intent to use it."

Brandon stopped short in his hunt for a wrench. "Uncle Jake, it's me. The third link broke and I'm trying to get the plows out of the field so I can get it fixed."

"Might as well buy a new one, because that Shuman ain't gonna get to it until next week sometime. Saw him at the barbershop on Monday, and he said he was backed up something awful."

"Yeah, well." Brandon hefted up the last of the tools he needed and swung the loop of chain on his shoulder. "Lucky for me we've got a sculptor next door."

"That Penelope's gonna weld it for you? Well, now. Good thinking." Uncle Jake stepped back from the doorway to let Brandon by.

"I didn't ask," he ground out. "She offered."

"Nice of her. But it sounds like you're running a quart low on gratitude, son."

Brandon discarded the words simmering in his brain and struggled for something Uncle Jake might not fuss about. "I'm grateful. But…"

"Hard to take help from a person you're trying to run off, eh?"

"I built her a barn, Uncle Jake!"

"Yeah. For the wrong reasons."

"It's still there. And look, see, it's paying off for me. The tractor broke down within an easy walk to it."

"Lucky you." Uncle Jake followed Brandon back out into the sunlight.

"What do you expect, anyway?" Brandon protested. "Me to just let it go? Me to be happy about it?"

Uncle Jake jammed his hands into the pockets of his overalls and kicked at a rock. "See, now, that's what most folks would advise. Get over it. Move on. But I know you.

And you are not the type to do that. It gnaws at you—no, no, don't think I don't see it."

Brandon adjusted the chain so it didn't bite into his shoulder. "Can we save this lecture for later? I have to go in at three today, and I want to get some sleep first, but I also want to make sure Penelope doesn't make a hash out of that repair. I don't want to be late for work. At a job, I might add, I had to go to full-time after Murphy stole *your* land. It's a lot easier to farm when you work part-time as a deputy rather than *full*-time."

"Things don't stay the same, Brandon. I want that land back, I won't lie. But I am not, *not,* y'hear, gonna become the same as Murphy to get it. Life is all on the—"

"All on the wheel, what goes around comes around. Yes, sir, I know that. You say it a thousand times. But maybe I don't want to wait for Murphy to get what's coming to him. Maybe I want to help him along."

Uncle Jake shook his head. "Yeah, but Brandon, you're forgetting something."

"What?"

"That bit about life being on the wheel? Well, what *you* dish out's gonna come back to haunt you. And I might add, be careful what you wish for. It has a habit of coming true."

Uncle Jake marched away, stiff legged, toward his pigpen. "Hold up there, Geraldine," he called out to the squealing hogs. "I'm coming. Yes, ma'am, I am on my way."

CHAPTER FOURTEEN

PENELOPE BENT over the link, trying to focus on her welding and not on the man who stood glowering at her from the open barn door.

Maybe he thinks I'm going to sabotage it.

More likely Brandon simply had doubts about her ability. He might know how to plow a field, but she knew more than a little about welding.

The first part done, she flipped up her welding hood and surveyed her work. "Not bad. Haven't lost my touch with cast iron," she pronounced.

Brandon came to stand beside her and inspected the weld. "Wow. Shuman wouldn't have done half as neat a job. I guess…" He trailed off, his cheeks reddening.

"Like I said. My pleasure. Now, I have to wrap this in blankets and let it cool, but the big part's done. I'll check it later."

"Where…? Who taught you how to weld?"

"Would you believe I learned how in college? I had to for an art class I was taking. It was…I don't know. I did it that semester, and I was hooked." She busied herself with wrapping the blankets around the part. "I thought my mom would stroke out when I told her I'd changed my major to art. She and Dad had sent me to college so I could get a degree in accounting and come back to join the family real estate business. Mom told me if all I wanted to do was learn how to weld, she could have sent me to a technical school and not wasted the money."

"Ouch."

"That's my mom. She worries, that's all. It's not a normal week if she doesn't email me at least three jobs she's found for me on some career site."

"But you could make good money welding. So why do they worry?"

Penelope chuckled, then closed the flap on the last blanket and turned to clear her workspace before answering. "I guess they can't bear to see their only daughter in the rough-and-tumble world of construction. They've been in real estate so long they have a taste of what that's like. And really, welding just to weld doesn't excite me."

"What does—" Brandon cleared his throat "—excite you?"

"Seeing something bigger than me—both in physical size and metaphoric meaning—come to life and know that I had something to do with it. Seeing an idea of mine that was once on paper become real. Don't you feel the same way about farming?" She stared at him.

"How do you mean?"

"Well, you go out there at the crack of dawn, presumably after a full night's work of being a deputy, and you molly-coddle that dirt. And then you plant seeds and you wait and wait for something to come up. But when it's harvest time, don't you feel proud of the work you've put in? That you had a hand in making it a reality?"

"Hmm. You put it that way…" Brandon raised his eyebrows and nodded slightly. "Yeah. I do. I feel real lucky, though, because sometimes I feel as though I've succeeded in spite of everything."

"Oh, I know about that!" Penelope tossed

him a push broom. "Here, sweep up that slag over there, will you?"

He started pushing the debris into a pile.

Penelope thought about her mother's repeated pleas for her to sell out and come home, about her dad's continuous refrain that she'd never be able to pay the house off. "The worst part is that sometimes..." She closed the box of welding rods and shut the storage cabinet doors. "Sometimes I think they're happy when I fail, you know? Sometimes I believe they don't want me to make it."

Brandon didn't reply at first. She looked over to see if he'd heard her and realized he was pushing his broom over an already clean part of the floor.

"Crazy, huh?" She laughed. "I tend to get morose when I get three no-thank-yous in one day. But it will happen."

"You mean three no-thank-yous on your project? In one day?"

"Part of the deal. You grow a thick skin. And sculpting is even worse than other media. But I know—I believe, anyway—if I can just get that first big break, I can make a living off it. I won't be rich. But I'll be doing what I want to do, and I don't need much more than that to make me happy."

"If you can't make a go of it welding for art, you've got a future in construction somewhere," Brandon told her. "You won't starve, that's for sure."

"Thanks."

"No, thank you. I wasn't exaggerating about you saving me a week. And I've been a real…you haven't, uh, caught me at my best today. So I guess I should be doubly grateful that you helped me out. Are you sure I can't pay you?"

"For what?" She took off her welding apron and reached to put it on its hook. Everything had its place—a place she'd picked out, that she'd decided on—and that pleased her.

"Shuman sure would have soaked me. I could pay you what I would have paid him."

For a moment, Penelope was tempted. But then she swept her eyes around her studio and the new home Brandon had made for her equipment. She shook her head. "The welding rods cost maybe two bucks. And my time, that's on the house. But if you really want to pay me back, pass the word to your farming buddies that I'm hanging out my shingle as a welder."

"Well, if you're sure—"

Just then, Penelope heard a noise outside the barn.

"Penny-girl! You here?"

BRANDON'S GUT TWISTED at the sound of Murphy's voice. For a moment, he froze, trying to deal with the sour taste in his mouth.

For her part, Penelope looked... Well, not happy, that was for sure.

"Let me," she said, and gestured with an awkward hand toward the open door.

"By all means," Brandon replied, not caring that his tone was acid.

But as she moved for the door, Murphy barreled in. "Penny-girl, looked for you in the house and waited there for the longest, but you—"

"Grandpa Murphy, please don't—it bothers me that you just walk right in my house when I'm not there."

Murphy wasn't paying the slightest attention to Penelope. His gaze had locked on Brandon.

"What's he doing here?" Murphy snapped.

"Hey, it's a free country." Brandon forced himself to lean back against the wall of the barn. "And this isn't your land anymore. Not to say it *ever* was. So I don't need your permission to come here."

"She's my granddaughter, you—"

"Grandpa! Brandon!" Penelope inserted herself between the two of them. "Grandpa, I'm doing some welding for Brandon. Brandon, please remember that you're speaking to my grandfather. If you wouldn't speak to me that way, then don't to my grandfather."

"You'd better get your money from him up front," Murphy warned her. "That Wilkes bunch has a reputation for being deadbeats. Just ask the county."

Brandon leaped forward and would have punched Murphy if Penelope hadn't been standing between them. "We pay our bills. We just don't think it's right when we're told to pay them a second time. And at least my family doesn't have a reputation for being crooks and would-be murderers."

"Whoa! Brandon!" Penelope put a hand to his chest and pushed him back.

Murphy made a move to shove her aside. "I'm no murderer!"

"Grandpa!" Penelope stumbled from her grandfather's push, and Brandon reached out to steady her.

"Take your hands off my granddaughter!"

Penelope looked down at Brandon's hand on her arm. He took in her wide eyes, her heaving breath. "Brandon, Brandon, you'd better leave if you're going to make such wild accusations."

Brandon dropped his hand in disgust. "Wild accusations? About a man who left Ryan MacIntosh's grandfather to die of a heart attack in a field? What? He didn't tell you about that?"

For a moment, Brandon thought he'd reached her. She put her fingers to her mouth and turned to Murphy.

"Tell her, Murphy! Tell her what happened that day!"

"You don't know anything! You'll believe that lousy farmhand's story? You want to, don't you? You want to believe that about me because it's a lot easier to hate me." Murphy put his hands on Penelope's shoulders and stared into her eyes. "Penny-girl, honey, he's filling your head with nonsense. He's trying to confuse you! Of course I didn't leave MacIntosh to die. I wasn't even there. Why would I do something like that? How could you even think that?"

When Penelope turned back to Brandon, her eyes were dark with anger. "Leave. Now."

"Penelope, you have to believe me."

"I don't have to do anything, Brandon. Tell me, who would you believe? Me? Or your uncle Jake?" A cold smile touched her lips. "Yeah. That's what I thought. So don't tell me I have to believe anything you say about Grandpa."

For a moment, Brandon wanted to press his argument. Having Penelope not believe him ripped something inside him.

But then an icy-hot fury filled him. "Fine. You want it that way? That's fine by me."

With that, he stalked past Murphy and left without so much as a backward glance.

PENELOPE SANK onto a stool at one of her workbenches and dropped her face into her hands.

"Well, that's good riddance to bad rubbish," Grandpa Murphy pronounced. "I told you not to let him hang around. What's he been telling you about me, anyway?"

"Nothing, Grandpa. Nothing. What did you need?"

"I can't come by and see you just because I want to?"

She looked up at the hurt in his voice. "I didn't mean it like that."

"Good thing I did come by. Tells you what kind of sheriff's department we have here, them letting the likes of him carry a badge." Grandpa yanked out a stool across from Penelope. "You mark my words, Penny-girl, he's not any sort you need to have. You need something, you come to me. I've still got a few friends in this town. No thanks, I might add, to Brandon Wilkes."

Her heart rate began to settle, leaving a pounding headache in its wake. "What was he talking about? About you leaving someone to die?"

Grandpa Murphy spit in disgust.

Penelope stood and crossed the room to him. "Why would anyone say something like that? Where did he get the idea that you would do something like that?"

"How should I know? He hates me. He's hated me from the day I bought his uncle's land. I try to help out a man. I'm there with ready cash and give him enough to get out of a bind—of his own making, mind you—and what thanks do I get? A promise from Brandon Wilkes that I'd live to regret it. And I sure have. It's because of Ryan MacIntosh and him that the government thinks I was involved in trying to defraud my crop insurance. There's no telling what they've said to the FBI, and now the feds are breathing down my neck, threatening to put me behind bars. If I had it to do over again..."

"You couldn't know, Grandpa. How could you know?"

"You're right. But buying this land, trying to help that ingrate Jake Wilkes, was the worst mistake I ever made."

Penelope patted him on the arm. "Not the worst. It brought me here, didn't it?"

He winked. "Got that right, sugar. And we'll make lemonade out of this old lemon yet."

CHAPTER FIFTEEN

"PRENTICE…Prentice, you can't…" Brandon swapped his PB&J for his cell phone and leaned back against the poplar. A breeze ruffled his hair, welcome after the morning he'd had.

I should never have given him that toy badge.

"You said I was a real, live deputy, Brandon! I's just helping out, is all. They was shoplifting. They was going to take that steak, and you know how expensive steak is."

Brandon hadn't had steak in so long that the mention of it made his mouth water. The PB&J he was eating turned to cardboard in his mouth. A steak, with all the trimmings, and Penelope smiling across from him…

He'd steered clear of her since the altercation with Murphy. It hadn't been that difficult, actually. Penelope had left the repaired part on her back step, complete with an invoice with a balance of zero.

Since then, the only time he'd seen her was from a distance, spying on him.

Although he wasn't sure if she'd seen that he'd started taking down, post by post, the fence Murphy had put up. Well, correct that, Murphy's workers. Murphy wouldn't know hard work if it bit him on the butt.

"Well, Prentice, you're a deputy in training. And even a shoplifter could have been dangerous. I know you saw them, but next time tell the manager before you go tackling a customer in the frozen food aisle. Okay? Promise?"

Prentice grumbled but finally conceded that he would follow Brandon's advice.

"Just until I get trained. But when I get a gun, Brandon, I'll be ready, won't I?"

Brandon shuddered at the thought. "You concentrate on getting in shape. How about I help you set up an obstacle course this weekend?" He really didn't need to be babysitting Prentice.

Was this the universe's way of telling Brandon he shouldn't be tearing down somebody else's fence? He didn't need to be indulging in revenge. He needed to get his uncle's winter wheat in the ground and then turn his attention to those strawberry plants he'd ordered.

He stared at the hateful fence, and inspiration struck. "Hey, I've got a better idea, one that will get you in shape and give you spending money. How would you like to help me finish tearing down a fence and plant some strawberries this weekend?"

Should he involve Prentice in this? Should he be taking the fence down at all?

Adverse possession. It's the only way you'll ever get this land back.

He squelched his conscience by reminding himself of Penelope's ice-cool reaction to the idea that her precious Grandpa Murphy could ever have harmed anyone. She'd never bend on this. No, the fence was coming down.

Brandon would pay Prentice a fair wage, and it would keep him out of trouble. Prentice was a natural at destroying things, so the fence should be right up his alley. With Prentice's help, that fence would be down in half the time it would take by himself.

That means Penelope might not notice it gone in time to do anything.

He forestalled Prentice's solemn oaths that he would work harder than a Transformer superhero robot. "Hey, no problem, Prentice, but I've gotta go. I have this day off and then the weekend, and I've got to make the most of it."

With Prentice's goodbyes echoing in his ears, he flipped shut the cell phone, crumpled up the plastic sandwich bag and tucked it in the cab of his truck.

He'd nearly reached the end of the branch separating the two parcels of land, where the copse of woods ended and the open field began. Part of the reason he'd made such progress tearing down the fence was that Murphy's workers had done a sorry job of putting it up to begin with. Half the posts it should have had, and half the wire fasteners.

Sean Courtland, the FBI agent, gave him confidence that as long as Brandon had permission, even verbal permission, to use the land, his claim of adverse possession wouldn't hold up in court.

He yanked on the metal fence post, feeling it struggle against the hold of the ground. But then it gave way and he tossed it onto the growing pile. These and the fence wire Brandon would return to Penelope. He wasn't a thief.

Just a trespasser.

Brandon paused for a rest, trying to sort out his emotions. All Penelope had to do was sell him the land back—at a loss to her, sure—and promise none of the money would go to Murphy. Brandon could live with that. That would settle things up.

Or would it? It's not enough, is it? You want her to admit what a rotten person Murphy is.

His cell phone buzzed in his pocket, and he reached for it to see it was the sheriff's department. Groaning, he answered it.

"Hey, got a call from that girl out by your Uncle Jake's. She's not happy," Wade told him.

"What now?"

"Something about you conspiring to drive her crazy?"

"I haven't talked to her in two days, no, make that three."

"She's on the phone now, and she wants to talk to you, pronto. Something about porcine trespass. What is porcine trespass anyway?"

Trespass. So it is the fence. Brandon's heart sank. "Can you patch her through?"

"It would be my privilege, buddy, just to get this problem off my plate and onto yours."

A few crackles and missed cues later, Wade said, "Ma'am? You can go ahead now."

"Penelope?" Brandon prompted when he didn't hear anything. "Penelope, are you—"

"I'm nose to nose with a hog," she said.

"What?"

"A big white hog with a black stripe around its neck. Ring any bells? It's in my yard. And I think it wants to come in the house."

"Shoo." Penelope closed her cell phone and slid it into her pocket. "Shoo." She waved a stick at the hog, which didn't seem disconcerted in the least by it.

The hog advanced a step or two, and Penelope retreated. Was there such a thing as stampeding swine? No point in taking chances. She eased up her back steps.

Leave it to Brandon to tell her to keep an

eye on the thing. He had no compunction whatsoever about expecting her to tackle jobs she had no clue how to do.

Like pig-sit.

"Don't even think about it," she told the hog as it nosed toward her. "Brandon said he was coming. Any minute now, he'll pull up and you'll be heading back to your pen."

Her cell phone buzzed, which seemed to interest the hog, and it closed the gap between them by one more delicate step. Penelope was running out of porch steps, and fast.

"Brandon?" she said into the phone, not bothering to check the caller ID. "You'd better come get this hog, and I mean now."

"Hog? My sister is tending swine? Talk about the prodigal son—uh, daughter."

"Trent." A heaviness that had nothing to do with her present predicament settled over her. Other people had normal relationships with their brothers, but she had never escaped the weight of comparison her parents dumped on her. Maybe if she'd once come up on the winning side of that competition her parents forced her into with her older brother.

"So you're really keeping pigs company down there in Alabama?"

"Georgia. It's Georgia."

"I knew that. Listen, I have news."

"Uh-huh?" She kept a vigilant eye on the hog as it snuffled in her petunias. Well, that was five bucks wasted, she thought, as the pig nibbled at the purple blossoms.

"I'm getting married."

"What?"

"Yep. Jill and I are tying the knot."

Jill: tall, willowy, very blond. Come to think of it, a carbon copy of all the women Trent dated.

"Well, congrats, Trent! I wish you much happiness. When's the big day?"

"That's the thing. See, they're having this big real estate conference in Maui next month, so we figured let's get married before then and go there for the honeymoon."

The hog munched on a few more petunia blossoms. Where on earth was Brandon? "You're going on a real estate conference for your honeymoon?"

"It was Jill's idea."

Oh, yeah. Jill was in real estate, too. Penelope had forgotten. Was the whole world in real estate?

"Then it sounds perfect," she said. She glared at the hog, who met her eyes with a look of unconcern.

"But Mom wants the wedding, you know?"

Penelope stifled a groan. She knew where this was heading, and it was the last place she wanted to go. "The wedding?"

"Yeah, nothing big, a couple of bridesmaids, a maid of honor, a flower girl. Maybe a couple hundred people."

"Uh-huh." If she didn't bite, would he go trolling for some other hapless bridezilla victim?

"So, uh, she wants to know, you know, your measurements."

"My what?"

"For your bridesmaid's dress. We've got to get a move on if we're going to make that Maui conference."

"Oh, no, no. Listen, you guys go ahead."

"Mom wants it. She insists."

"She can *un*-insist. I don't even know Jill. I'm really happy for you, don't get me wrong.

But I have zero desire, zilch, to be a bridesmaid. No offense."

"None taken. But…"

Behind her, Penelope heard Theo's plaintive yowl. He'd obviously spotted her out the window, which meant he was on the *verboten* kitchen counter, and he was jealous of her conversation with the hog.

"But what, Trent? Tell her thanks, but no thanks."

"Mo-om! She said no!"

"Oh, good grief, is she listening?"

But Penelope's question was answered by her mother herself. "Penelope! I can't believe you value your brother so little that you refuse to participate."

"Mom, listen. I'm kind of busy right now." The hog nosed ever closer to Penelope, and she backed up to the top step.

"What on earth is that sound?"

"It's a hog. Snuffling."

"A hog?"

"I did say I was busy."

"Oh, Penelope. Why must you be so dramatic?"

A vehicle rattled up the driveway and

Penelope could've collapsed with relief. Brandon!

But it wasn't. It was Brandon's uncle, his truck outfitted with a strange set of fence pieces along the back. Hopefully to keep the pig in?

"Hey, there," he greeted her. "Geraldine, what on earth are you doin' eatin' those petunias? You know they give you heartburn."

"...expect you to be here," her mother was saying in an imperious tone. "And if you don't have a date, I'll need to know that, too, because all the ushers they've chosen are married. I'll find someone suitable."

Weddings and hogs. What a combination. Somehow Penelope could stomach the hog more easily than the idea of swathing herself in whatever hideous bridesmaid color was this season's hot pick. "Mom. I gotta go. The man's here to pick up his pig."

CHAPTER SIXTEEN

"Aw, HONEY, now you know better than this. You know you're not supposed to be off loafin'." Brandon's uncle reached down and rubbed Geraldine behind the ear.

Penelope did a double take as the hog leaned into the scratch. Jake Wilkes grinned.

"Pigs make great pets. They're right smart critters."

"Uh-huh, Mr. Wilkes." She couldn't quite mask her disbelief.

"Oh, don't bother being so formal. Everybody just calls me Uncle Jake. I sure am sorry about your petunias. I'll see about getting you some more. Geraldine just loves 'em better 'n candy."

"I never knew pigs ate…" She trailed off.

"Anything but slop? I know. Lots of people don't know that. I wouldn't mind her eatin' flowers, but it does give her heartburn, and then she just sorrows around all day. I think it's 'cause she pigs out on 'em, no pun intended."

"Well, thank you for getting her," Penelope said. "I was working out in the barn, and I looked up and saw her."

"Yep. The others got out, and Miss Geraldine was lonesome. I'm worn out from herding them back up and in the pen. I can't think how Miss Geraldine got way over here, what with that fence between us. Now, I know, I know—" he held up his hand "—you're gonna say that hogs go through fences like a rat goes through cheese, but Miss Geraldine's usual limit is one fence a day."

Penelope hadn't planned on saying anything as colorful as that.

Uncle Jake hooked his fingers into the overall straps. "They are a lot of trouble, though, gotta admit that. Always getting out and getting into somebody's something or 'nother. Brandon keeps telling me I should get rid of 'em…but it'd be like, well… I'm down to just my favorites. Don't really take any to market anymore. And what would I do to keep busy, you know? Since my heart started giving me trouble, Brandon don't like me doing a lot of plowing and such. That boy is a professional worrier, you ask me."

Penelope gave into the temptation to hear more about Brandon. "I guess it's the law enforcement part of him."

Uncle Jake chuckled. "No, ma'am, that's the farmer in him. I did a bad thing, letting him ride a tractor that first time. Boy took to it like Geraldine took to those petunias of yours. I tell him he oughta loosen up, and lately it does seem as if he's taking my advice. Or maybe you're prettier to hang around than me."

She couldn't hold back her laughter. "Thank you for the compliment, but Brandon's not been hanging around here. That field has been taking up all his time."

"So you're a sculptor, huh?" Uncle Jake asked after an awkward silence. He propped one elbow on the porch railing, his frail chambray shirtsleeve protesting at the strain. Geraldine ambled over toward a clump of dandelions.

Mindful of all the questions about her art she'd fielded in the past by well-meaning but clueless people, Penelope answered with a cautious, "I try to be."

"No, now, don't sell yourself short. An artist's either an artist or he's not. Have I maybe seen pictures of your work?"

She shook her head. "Probably not. I've done some small-scale pieces for a few businesses and individuals, and my work has been in some galleries in L.A. and New York, but this project I was working on was my first big break. I really thought..." She clamped her mouth shut.

"You and Brandon, y'all are quite the pair." Jake took his cap off and wiped his forehead.

"What do you mean?"

"You got that same look in your eye. It's like y'all think it's your job to take over the world or somethin'. Like y'all believe it's up to you to take life and squeeze it into the shape of whatever dreams have caught your fancy. Ambitious, both of you."

Penelope hated to admit sharing a character trait with Brandon, least of all ambition. He was someone who let his ambitions for revenge blind him.

Jake shifted his weight from one worn

leather brogan to the other. "Mind if I take a gander at this thing you're working on?"

"Uh…" Penelope sat on the step and stared at the man leaning on her porch. His question surprised her. Ordinarily she didn't like strangers staring over her shoulder as she worked. It woke her inner critic.

"Just curious, is all. Brandon doesn't say much about it."

"That's probably because I haven't got much done on it. I've only really just started."

"So are you, what, postmodern, then, I guess? I'm a modern guy myself. I was always kind of partial to Henry Moore's stuff."

Penelope did a double take. "You know Henry Moore's work?"

Uncle Jake took out a pocketknife. Apparently absorbed in the task of trimming his nails, he said, "Well, never saw any of it in real life. But pictures, yeah. I like how simple it looks, just the bare essentials, enough for you to imagine the rest. And I like all those piercings and holes he put in. Reminds me that human beings aren't whole without somebody to love."

"I'd never thought of his work in quite that

way, but, yeah, you have a point." Penelope tried to hide her amazement by fidgeting with the hem of the leather welder's apron she wore.

"I was hoping you were coming along with it. I figure seeing a big sculpture like that for real is kind of like hearing live music. First time I ever heard an orchestra play, I felt those bass drums rumble right down in my chest. Ain't nothing like it."

"Well…" Penelope scrutinized him for any signs of false flattery. She made her decision. "I'll show you what I've got so far." She struck off for the barn, stopped and glanced back at Geraldine.

"Aw, she won't bother anything. She's happy and them dandelions will ease that stomach of hers."

Penelope smothered a laugh. "Okay. If you're sure."

In the shop, she pulled out the pieces she'd been working with on the English wheel, thin strips of stainless steel she'd carefully formed into wavy ribbons. "This will be the top of it."

"Man. I like that. That sure is pretty. And

look at that welding. I'll bet you could do some mighty fine bodywork on a car. I ever get in a fender-bender, I'll just bring the old thing to you, how 'bout it." Uncle Jake ran a finger along the mirror-bright finish. "That thing'll glitter like a dime-store window when you get it all put together and the sun hits it."

She nodded approvingly. "That's the reason I'm going with stainless steel. It's harder to work with, though, and of course I have to be careful handling it so I don't mar the finish."

"'Course."

A rap on the barn door made them both look back. Brandon stood there, not exactly smiling, but not wearing the grouchy expression he had so much around her. "Hey. Swine-removal services have arrived."

Penelope ordered herself not to be so glad, but her heart was as obedient as a spoilt child.

"Thanks, I wasn't sure what to do with a pig."

"I saw she got your petunias. What are you guys talking about in here?"

Was that suspicion in Brandon's voice?

Overprotection at the very least, and Penelope well knew what overprotective love sounded like.

"You seen this?" Uncle Jake gestured at the ribbons of steel. "Ain't this something?"

Brandon walked over to take a closer look. "I've seen a model, but it looks different when it's this big. Those ripples remind me of water."

Penelope smiled. "That's it! That's exactly what I wanted—these will be my interpretations of the man and woman in the piece. I'm having to weld pieces together after I've formed them. Oh, I'm so glad you…"

She didn't finish her thought. They understood her art, but did that mean they would applaud it? Or support it? Or at least not get in her way?

But just understanding and appreciation was a change. Her mother, perfectionist that she was, would have said, "Honey, wouldn't it have looked nicer flat and smooth? Why have all those wrinkles in it? It looks like it needs ironing."

Her father would have pooh-poohed the waste of quality stainless steel. And Trent would have said something smarmy about the whole concept, but that's what older brothers did, right?

Brandon returned her grin, but suddenly he seemed to retreat into his deputy persona, despite his dusty T-shirt and blue jeans. His expression was nothing beyond politeness.

"Is something wrong?" she asked.

He hesitated. "Just tired from working, and the call from the sheriff's department—"

"You're off today!" Uncle Jake exploded. "What's he want, anyway, you to pull another extra shift?"

"No, no, Uncle Jake. I'm off. The sheriff's department called me about Geraldine. It's okay, no extra shifts today. I'm just glad I got here in time to help you load Geraldine."

"What? Me? Need help loading a hog? Been doin' it all my life. Don't need any such molly-coddling."

Penelope smothered a chuckle as Brandon rolled his eyes. She caught his gaze and he gave her a pointed shake of his head, as if to say, *What can you do?*

"And speaking of which, I guess I'd better load the ol' girl and get going."

Penelope and Brandon followed Uncle Jake
out into the bright sunshine. Penelope looked
from the hog to Uncle Jake. "How do you
plan on getting her on the truck?"

"Oh, that's easy enough. I been training
her." Uncle Jake walked over and dropped
the tailgate. He yanked out a wide plank and
rigged up a ramp. With two fingers to his
lips, he forced out a shrill whistle through his
teeth. The hog jerked her head up and stared
in her master's direction. He stretched out
an arm and pointed to the back of the truck.

Penelope could've sworn the hog looked
downcast.

Geraldine dipped her head back for another dandelion, and Uncle Jake whistled
again. This time, he added in a stern voice,
"I mean it, Geraldine. On the truck now. Fun
and games are over for you."

To Penelope's amazement, the hog shuffled
over and picked her way up the ramp.

"That's incredible! If I had a video of that,
we could—"

"'T'ain't nothin." Uncle Jake slammed the
tailgate shut. "Raised that hog on a bottle,
from the time she was barely able to suck.

She's always been on the runty side, but she's sharp, that one."

Brandon laughed. "I think 'that one' outgrew her runt status a long time ago, Uncle Jake. Need any help getting her back in the pen?"

"Nope." Uncle Jake checked the tailgate. "Best get her home now. Will I see you for supper? Penelope, you're welcome to come, too."

The captive Geraldine began to grunt in the back of the truck. "All right, all right. We're going. But who's the one that run off and eat up somebody else's petunias, huh?" He reached in and gave the hog a pat.

Beside Penelope, Brandon shook his head. "I think I'll grab something from town and fix supper at my place."

"Yeah, you'll run into that sheriff of ours, and he'll say you need to write a couple dozen reports, and oh, by the way, somebody's called in sick, so can you maybe pull their shift?"

But Uncle Jake apparently wasn't expecting an answer. He slammed the door shut behind him and pulled off, still grumbling.

Penelope let out the laugh she'd been holding back. "Your uncle is priceless! Pigs and sculptures? I would have never guessed he was a fan of Henry Moore's!"

"Henry who?"

"A famous sculptor—oh, never mind." She wasn't going to let an art appreciation lecture ruin the moment. "Thanks for coming. I had my mom on the phone telling me I was drafted for bridesmaid duty *again* and Geraldine eating up all my petunias."

"A wedding, huh? Who's getting married?"

"My brother. I'm going to try—"

But her cell phone buzzed in her pocket.

She snagged it and flipped it open, not even getting a greeting out before her mother snapped, "Are you done with your barnyard animals now?"

"Mom, you make it sound—"

Her mother modulated the irritation out of her voice, which told Penelope just how irritated she was. "Penelope, sweetheart, I know you don't like weddings, and yes, it does mean a flight home, but I don't think it would be that much of a burden for you. It is your *only* brother's wedding, after all."

Penelope turned and walked away from Brandon. "Mom, of course I'm coming to the wedding. You know I wouldn't miss Trent's wedding." She tried not to think about the hit her finances would take for the flight out at such short notice.

"Good, then. Trent said you didn't want to be a bridesmaid, and I couldn't imagine you not—"

Now how to get out of the bridesmaid business? "Mom, does *Trent* want me to be a bridesmaid?"

Her mother scoffed. "Trent is a man. He doesn't know the first thing about a wedding. If he did, would he have agreed to have it in two weeks? Of course you have to be one of Jill's bridesmaids. It would look awful if you weren't included."

"Does *Jill* want me to be a bridesmaid?" The idea that someone she'd met only once or twice wanted her to serve such an integral part in her big day blew Penelope's mind. But if it was important to her brother's future wife, then so be it.

"*Jill* wanted to do the wedding in blue jeans and bare feet. Her mother and I put a stop to that pronto. Your brother has already added to my stress. Do you realize how impossible it is to put together a wedding in that time? Jill's mother is going completely crazy, and I'm pitching in, but still it's—"

Penelope bit her lip to keep back the giggle at the image of her mother "pitching in." Probably a good portion of the mother-of-the-bride's stress was Penelope's mother's "pitching in."

"Are you laughing? Penelope Langston, are you snickering?"

Penelope bit down harder. "Mom, have you ever considered, just for the briefest of nano-seconds, that maybe Trent and Jill don't want a big wedding?"

"But they'll regret it, Penelope! They'll only have one shot at this and they will so regret it. I know. I'm your mother, and I know these things. So please. Please. Don't be difficult now."

"It's just that I'm not really fired up about being a bridesmaid. But, yeah. I guess I'll do it." Another hit to the bank account. Maybe she could talk Jill back into the blue jeans idea. "Have you spoken to Grandpa? I'll need to get his ticket as well."

Silence. "I'm not inviting your grandfather."

"What?"

"You heard me. Your grandfather and I have not… It's just too difficult, Penelope. He would make a hash out of everything. All he does is use people and manipulate their better instincts. I've warned you about him, and you refuse to listen."

"Mom, you cannot seriously expect me to drop everything and fly out to be a bridesmaid for my brother's total stranger of a fiancée, all because it's his only shot at the 'big day,' and then not invite Grandpa Murphy?"

"You know how it is with your grandmother. She refuses to be in the same room with him. And I have to side with her on this. She has excellent reasons. And if you have any feelings for your grandmother, respect her wishes, not to mention mine. Can't you simply trust us that we know best? Besides," her mom said, adopting a placating tone, "he's not really been a big part of our lives."

"Because you refused to make him a part, Mom! How could he be? How can he now? He's a sick old man, and this is his only grandson's wedding day. If it's important enough for me to be there, then it's even more—"

"Don't try guilting me. Your grandfather does that perfectly well. Oh. And I know you don't have the money to buy a plane ticket. So your father and I are buying it. Don't get all stiff-necked. I'll talk to you tomorrow with all the details. And Penelope..." Her mother trailed off and then added with an unbending firmness, "don't make things difficult by insisting on your grandfather being there."

With that, her mother hung up.

CHAPTER SEVENTEEN

For a moment Penelope stood there with the cell phone at her ear, listening to the silence. She could not believe her mother had hung up on her.

Her stomach churned as she closed the phone. How was she going to explain to Grandpa Murphy that he was persona non grata at Trent's wedding? He had been trying so hard these past few weeks to make up for the years he'd not been able to be around.

With the allusions he'd made to phone conversations with her mom, Penelope had hoped that the old family feud between them, whatever had caused it, was fading.

Guess that was wishful thinking.

"Sounds like some family drama there."

Brandon. Penelope had forgotten he was there. She realized she was gripping the phone so hard it dug into her palm. Slipping it into her pocket, she pressed her lips together and turned on him. "And it's none of your business, thank you very much."

"Oh, I don't know. Anything to do with Murphy is very much my business. I like to keep an eye on him."

"You—you—" Penelope pressed her thumb and forefinger to her eyes. Another day, another headache. "My grandfather's right. You make him out to be some sort of monster so it's easier for you to hate him. If you could just see him the way I see him. If you could know him the way I know him."

Brandon chuckled, the sound bitter and hollow. "Funny. I was thinking the exact same thing. And it sounds as though, at least from your end of the conversation with your mother—it was your mother, wasn't it?" He paused but didn't wait long enough for her to answer. "Well, it sounds as if she had the brains to keep you away from him when you were younger."

Penelope gritted her teeth. "Like I said, my family disagreements are none of your business."

"But this irrational attachment you have for—"

"For my grandfather? It's no more irratio-nal for me to love my grandfather, warts and all, than it is for you to love your uncle, who was the actual one to cause you to lose this precious land. I don't see you yelling accu-sations at *him*."

Brandon's face went white and he walked stiffly past her.

"Wait! Brandon, I'm sorry, that was un-called-for." Penelope made a grab for his arm, but he shook her off him. She stepped in front of him.

"Brandon! You cannot stomp away from disagreements every time."

He glared down at her. "It's better than say-ing what I think."

"Okay, so I am not the most tactful of peo-ple. I know that. But you don't have the mar-ket cornered on tact, either. You find some way of needling me every time we meet. And you could obviously see I was having a con-versation that was meant to be private. I'm sorry, but it really… violated my privacy."

"You don't seem to be able to enforce those boundaries with your grandfather. It ought to tell you something that he comes in your house without permission, even when he knows it bothers you."

She blew out an exasperated breath. "See? That's what I mean. You pick up these arcane bits of information about me and then you turn around and use them against me. I feel manipulated."

"Hey," Brandon said, holding up his hands. "I'm just pointing out the truth. If I were manipulating you, I'd take a page out of Richard Murphy's book."

"You know, when you're not running down my grandfather, you can be a really nice guy. So why can't we just agree to disagree on this and not bring Grandpa Murphy up?"

"Oh, right, let's ignore the elephant in the corner, shall we?"

"I only meant that, for instance, on the tractor, we had fun, didn't we? And when I was welding… And earlier, when I was showing you and your uncle the work I'd done on my sculpture. It's good when we find common ground."

Brandon didn't answer immediately. He looked off in the distance, his eyes dark and inscrutable. "Why is it so important that I like you?" he asked finally.

"Because, honestly, you're the first person I've ever clashed with. Well, except my mom, but you know moms." She laughed, embarrassed. It didn't relieve the tension.

Penelope took a deep breath and started again. "As I was saying, I'm not the world's most popular person, granted, but people usually don't hiss and spit around me. I've never known someone who, well, it's as though you're constantly taking out your dislike of my grandfather on me. Whatever the trouble—"

"My *dislike* of your grandfather?" Brandon scoffed. "Honey, I don't just *dislike* Richard Murphy. I hate his guts. And I don't care how much he bounced you on his knee, I'll never see him as anything but the conniving, manipulative, greedy criminal he is."

She closed her eyes against the onslaught of his anger. This was never going to work, whatever it was that she was hoping for.

"Fine." Penelope turned away from him, too weary to argue. "Hate my grandfather, hate me. I don't care. I give up."

This time it was Brandon who caught her by the elbow. He pulled her back toward him. "I don't hate you, Penelope. I could never hate you. What makes you think that?"

She couldn't meet his eyes. "It's not too hard to figure out. You paint me with the same brush you paint my grandfather. And you're right. I don't know why it even matters what you think of me. The sun will rise, the earth will spin around, the sun will set no matter what your opinion."

He tipped her chin up. "*Hate* is a strong word. You frustrate me. That's true. You frustrate me in so many ways. You wouldn't believe the ways you frustrate me."

Penelope searched his face. "Brandon—"

"Shh. Just for a moment, let me forget who you are."

Brandon's fingers slid into her hair, cradling her head as he lowered his lips to hers. She put her palm against his chest, intending to stop him, but the moment his mouth was against hers, she couldn't think why on earth she wanted to stop anything that felt this good.

He pulled her to him and she let her hand

slide up to his neck, let him press against her. She could not get enough of the sensation of his mouth on hers. It was as though she was a starving woman and he'd offered her a piece of bread. But the more she had, the hungrier she became.

Brandon stumbled backward, breaking the kiss, leaving her confused and bewildered.

"What—"

"I can't," he said. Misery pinched his features.

"You can't what?"

He put a hand to his face. "I can't forget who you are."

Then he turned and headed into the woods that separated her land from his uncle's.

BRANDON CURSED himself all the way to Murphy's fence. How could he have been so stupid as to kiss her? Crazy, just plain stupid and crazy.

He wrestled another stretch of fence wire away from the posts with the strength only frustration could give a man.

Forget her. It's just hormones and you need to think with your head.

A sharp prong of the wire dug into his hand, and he felt perverse relief. The pain was nothing compared to the agony when he'd kissed her.

The cut gushed blood. He got his first-aid kit out of the truck's glove compartment. Again, he welcomed the burning pain of the alcohol as he poured it over the wound.

For a moment, while he'd held Penelope, he'd felt...what? Not just the normal urges a guy had when he was kissing a woman as beautiful as Penelope, but something else, something far scarier. He'd felt as if she was worth letting everything else go.

Worth letting Murphy off the hook? No. Never. No one was worth that.

He gritted his teeth and flushed the cut with still more alcohol. Studying it, he decided it wasn't quite bad enough for stitches, but it would probably leave a scar.

Good. A scar will be a reminder of how close I came to forgetting my priorities.

"Brandon? Brandon Wilkes! Are you back here?"

Penelope. He set the bottle of alcohol on the truck seat so hard a little sloshed on the vinyl. He should have known she'd follow him. And now she'd see the fence, and knowing Penelope, she'd swear out a warrant for trespassing.

There goes your plan, buddy.

She came through the last of the brush between them with the fury of a tornado. "There you are! Listen, I am tired of this hot-and-cold business! First you act as though you hate my guts, and then you—"

She paused, for the first time looking around her. "What are you doing?" Her voice was small and quiet, almost overwhelmed by the woods around them.

Brandon swallowed. "Taking down the fence."

"That I see." The quietness was gone now, and in its place pure steel.

"You did say I could use the land."

"But I didn't say a thing about you taking down the fence!"

Better do some fast talking now, bud.

"Well…" In his head, Brandon ran through explanations and excuses and defenses, but just as quickly discarded them.

"Well? What?"

Unexpected shame coursed through him. This wasn't right, what he'd been doing. If Murphy had done something similar, Brandon would have ripped his heart out.

"It's hard to get the tractor in and out. Half the time, your car's in the way. And besides, it's stupid to waste time treating this as two fields when it's really supposed to be one field."

He could see the protest on her lips, in the angry way she stood, arms akimbo.

"You're expecting me to believe you did this just to be more efficient?"

Brandon riffled through the first-aid box for a large square of gauze. "I don't expect you to believe anything I say. Why should I think you'd start now? Wouldn't it just be a waste of breath?"

A beat or two of silence was the only response Brandon got. He heard twigs snap as she came closer to him. "You've hurt yourself."

"Yeah. Fence wire'll do that."

"Here. Let me. You'll never bandage it one-handed." She took his injured hand in her own, her fingers light on his skin.

She's worth more than Murphy.

He shook his head.

"Did I hurt you?" She looked up, and all he could do was stare into her brown eyes.

"No. But it does hurt."

Penelope took the gauze from him and began bandaging the cut, tearing the surgical tape with even white teeth.

He swallowed again as she stepped back and let go of his hand.

"I'd keep that dry. You sure you don't need stitches?"

"You're a one-woman superhero. I figured you would offer to stitch it up if I needed them."

"I'll take that as a no." Penelope turned back and studied the dismantled fence.

"I'll put it back if you want me to."

Now why had he offered that? If she said yes, he'd be duty-bound to do it. If she said no, then that was permission for him to have done it, which was another nail in the coffin of his adverse possession claim.

"I don't know what I want you to do." Pain rippled through her words, and suddenly

Brandon realized she was in as much conflict about the kiss as he'd been.

"The tractor—it would be easier," he managed to get out.

"That's how Geraldine got in my yard, isn't it?"

Brandon puzzled it out, looked up through the woods and saw the figure of Uncle Jake moving around in his yard. Uncle Jake had a much better vantage point to see what he'd been doing than Penelope would have from her house.

Through the trees, he saw his uncle staring back at him, or at least in his general direction. Brandon didn't doubt the old codger had let Geraldine loose to clue Penelope in about the downed fence. He sighed.

"I guess. I didn't see her come by, but I've taken up a lot of fence."

"If you had just asked. You're as bad as my grandfather, waltzing over boundaries and through doors. Why is it that people won't take my no for an answer? Not my parents, not Grandpa Murphy, not you. Especially not you! Just once, I want someone to hear me when I say no."

She burst into tears and stumbled back the way she'd come.

CHAPTER EIGHTEEN

THE RIDE OF THE VALKYRIES erupted out of Penelope's pocket as she hit the porch steps. She ignored it and rubbed away her tears to see to slide the key into her back door's lock.

Funny. In Oregon, her parents never felt the need to lock a door. The way their house was situated high on a hill, any intruder would have stuck out like a sore thumb. But here, in the middle of Nowhere, Georgia, she was having to take the same care to lock her doors as she did when she lived in New York.

But this time, ha-ha, it was against well-meaning grandfathers.

The lock gave way, surprising Theo from his slumber on the high shelf of a baker's rack she'd knocked together earlier in the week. He yawned hugely, inspected her for a few seconds, then curled back up into a ball.

"That was supposed to be a test for the welder, Theo. And I may have to sell it—

somewhere, though who knows where. So don't get used to that as a perch."

Theo didn't respond.

Right. Even her cat didn't listen to her. Penelope went for the bottle of aspirin. Shaking two pills out of the bottle, she tried to ignore how her fingers were trembling.

The water from the tap tasted clean and cool as it washed the tablets down. She'd never had such good water straight out of a tap. In New York, a filter was de rigueur, and even water back home in Oregon didn't taste this good. Finally she could understand why her mother pined for the water back in *her* home of Georgia.

Her mother. Penelope dialed her mother's number. Might as well get it over and done with.

Before Penelope could even get a greeting out, her mother was speaking. "I wanted to apologize for hanging up like that. It was rude and I'm sorry. I shouldn't have done it."

Penelope sank into one of the dinette chairs and propped her forehead in the palm of her hand, elbow on the table. "It's okay, Mom. We weren't going to accomplish any peace treaty if you hadn't hung up, so don't worry about it."

She heard her mother's long sigh.

"Penelope—"

"Mom, believe it or not, your hanging up on me is the least of my problems right now, okay? I have a horrid headache. Brandon Wilkes is tearing down my fence, and—" What else was there to say? Something straight out of a pity party about how even her cat refused to listen to her?

"Your fence? He's taking down your fence? Along your property line?"

"Well, he has always maintained there *is* no property line there, because he swears that Grandpa Murphy conspired in some way to force the land sale to begin with. Something about taxes and the tax commissioner. Oh, Mom, I don't know! He hates Grandpa Murphy and won't listen to reason."

Her mother chuckled drily. "Hmm. Seems to be the standard reaction to my father's shenanigans."

Penelope's stomach growled, forestalling the protest she was going to make. She looked up at the clock. It was after two o'clock, no wonder she had a headache. Rising to her feet, she started poking through the cabinets and the fridge for something quick.

"Penelope? Are you still there?"

"Yes, Mom. I'm here. I'm trying to score some lunch, that's all. I had the pig to deal with, which got in my yard because Brandon took the fence down, and then I—" She paused, thinking about Brandon's kiss.

"Then what?" Her mother waited a beat. "That's when you discovered the fence?"

"Yeah. Something like that." Whole-wheat bread, brown mustard, some of the sliced turkey breast, romaine and tomatoes she'd bought during her last grocery-store run. The phone still pressed to her ear, she pulled a butter knife out of the drawer.

"So you've confronted him about it?"

"Brandon? Oh, yeah." Back at the table, Penelope started assembling her sandwich, the phone tucked between her shoulder and her ear. "He says it's to make it easier to cultivate the fields. One big field would be easier than two, and all that."

"Well…" Her mother clucked sympathetically. "He's right about that. With two small fields, you spend half your time turning the tractor around and the other half on the road getting the tractor back and forth between the fields."

"Oh, Mom! You're not siding with him on this, are you? I mean, you're the one who always warns home owners to never let fences on property lines become compromised."

"You have a plat, right? Showing the boundaries? And a rental agreement describing how he can use the land?"

"Uh, not exactly. I mean, I have a verbal one. Don't start. I know I should have one in writing." She didn't want to confess to her mother that she'd let Brandon use the land for free. At the time, she'd bought into Brandon's pitiful-uncle story, but maybe that whole thing was just an act.

"Well, get one, dear," her mother said crisply. "In writing. And put in it that, at the expiration of the agreement, he has to restore the fence at his cost, and back to the original land line. Put in there as well that if it has to be resurveyed, he pays for those costs, too. If you want, fax a copy of the plats to me, and I'll draw one up."

For a moment, Penelope was tempted to refuse. But it was a sensible plan, and the best way to handle it. Her mother had expertise she didn't have, expertise that would cost her dearly if she went to an attorney here.

And if Brandon didn't want to sign the agreement, she'd have him prosecuted for trespassing.

"Okay. I'll fax up a copy of my deed. It will be easier than the plat, and it will have the boundaries on it," Penelope told her.

"Good. Now, about your grandfather."

"Mom, could we please—"

"I want to say my piece so my conscience will be clear. I'll have warned you the best I can, and I won't say another word."

"Mom, please—"

"There are things about your grandfather you don't know, things that I didn't tell you about when you were younger, because…" Her mother exhaled. "I don't know why, exactly. He wasn't really a problem when you were little because we were so far away, and far be it for my father to trouble himself to come see us. And then, well, he married that woman."

"Mom, you don't have to worry about Eileen. She left him when he lost everything this summer."

"Par for the course with that family. They were crooks from the word go, even if they did clean up well. I didn't care if my father remarried. That wasn't the point. Your grandmother had made her own life with us, and she was happy—far, far happier than she'd ever been with him. He's…your grandfather—"

"Mom!" Penelope interrupted more sharply than she'd intended, but it did the trick.

"Yes?"

"I don't want to hear this. To hear how you couldn't get along with Grandpa Murphy. I can get along with him and that's all I need to know."

"Oh, but Penelope, you can't. You may think you can, but it's because he's arranging things. Manipulating circumstances."

Penelope could visualize her mother's face, knitted with concern. She knew that expression. She'd been treated to it whenever she did something her mother thought was a poor choice—changing her major to art, going on to art school for her master's, living on a shoestring in first L.A. and then New York.

Oh, and don't forget the biggie: buying this land.

"Your grandfather can get nasty when he doesn't get his way, honey. I don't want to see you hurt, that's all. All these years, I didn't want you to know what a…"

Penelope waited for her mom to supply the insult of her choice. When the word didn't come, Penelope prompted. "What a what he was?"

"He's very cunning. Very slick. He's done things."

"What things, Mom? Tell me, if they're so awful."

"I don't want to. I know he's my father, but he can be a horrible, horrible man. I honestly don't even like to remember it. And he's got you so charmed that you're never going to believe it anyway, are you? Not until you see what he really is."

A long moment of silence stretched out. Penelope looked down at her uneaten sandwich and pushed it away. "Maybe he's changed?" she offered.

"For your sake, Penelope, I hope so. I hope so. Listen, I've got to go. I love you, and I'm glad you're coming home for Trent's wedding. I could use some help on it. Jill's mom has got a to-do list a mile long. She's even got a seating chart she's working on. A seating chart! Oh, well, I know how she feels. When you get married, I'll want the perfect wedding for you. I love you, honey. I don't always tell you that, but I do. And I...I hope I'm wrong about your grandfather. Maybe he *has* changed."

Were tears clogging her mother's throat? Penelope didn't get a chance to ask, because her mom clicked off a second later.

A MOCKINGBIRD SASSED somewhere high in a poplar tree above Brandon's head, and a squirrel jumped from branch to branch in an oak tree. Other than that, it was preternaturally quiet in the wake of Penelope's abrupt departure.

Boundaries. It all came down to boundaries. He gazed at the fence dispassionately and thought about Robert Frost's poem about good fences making good neighbors. How good a neighbor had he been to Penelope?

And why, since she was a Murphy, did it matter to him?

But it did. He'd wanted to go after her, put his arms around her and comfort her, swear that no one would intrude on her space again if he could help it. He'd stood there, though, feet nailed to the ground.

Should he put the fence back up? Or take it down? She hadn't said one way or the other. He'd hurt her and, beyond the obvious breach of trust, he'd hurt her in some deep way he couldn't understand.

His cell phone rang, and he snatched it out of his pocket, irritated.

"Brandon?" his uncle asked.

Oh, boy. Now, as if he didn't feel enough of a total heel, Uncle Jake was going to get in on the act.

"Yes, sir?"

"If you're at a stopping point on your so-called sneak attack on that there fence, Becca MacIntosh has some news for you. She's up here, wants to talk."

CHAPTER NINETEEN

BECCA WAS WAITING for him on the swing that hung from the old pecan tree. Brandon saw that Uncle Jake had gone all-out, with his best pitcher full of ice water and real glasses on the rickety table between the swing and the glider.

"You look plenty hot and tired," Becca said by way of greeting. "Can I interest you in a glass of your uncle's ice water?"

"I believe you can," Brandon said. He crossed over to the pitcher and poured himself a tall, cold glass. Out of the corner of his eye, he saw Uncle Jake leaning back in the glider.

"Good of you to come join us," his uncle said with just the slightest hint of sarcasm. "I know you been busy the whole day on that fence."

Brandon didn't respond right away, just took another swallow of water. Bringing the glass down from his mouth, he realized his uncle was still waiting for his reply.

"Yes, sir," he said simply.

"Don't know why you're fooling with that thing anyway," Uncle Jake went on, "not with us needing to get that winter wheat in the ground and them strawberry plants in, too. Time'd be better spent on planting, not tearing down a fence that wasn't bothering nobody."

"Uncle Jake, you know planting will go a lot quicker if I don't have to contend with that fence."

"Right, right, especially if you have to stop twice a day to help me get the hogs back in their pen after they've wandered off into Penelope's yard."

Brandon's suspicion that Uncle Jake had sent Geraldine on a mission was confirmed by the glint in the old man's eyes. He knew he could expect the hogs to be out every day until he settled this fence business once and for all.

Before he could say anything, though, Uncle Jake posed one more observation. "I guess you *did* get permission from Penelope before you started vandalizing her property, what with you being a sheriff's deputy and knowing the law and whatnot."

Brandon looked over at Becca, who was trying in vain not to laugh at Uncle Jake's doggedness.

"She knows," he said, not elaborating.

"Well, now, that's good, that's real good." Uncle Jake took a swig of his water and beamed at first Brandon and then Becca. "I knew my nephew wasn't the trespassing type. Don't know why I spent the morning worrying about it. Guess we can concentrate on what news you've brought us, Becca."

Becca set her glass down on the table. "I've got good news and I've got bad news."

"Bad," Brandon said.

"Good," his uncle said at the same time. He grinned up at Brandon. "Makes the medicine go down."

Becca laughed. "I suppose, since you fellows can't seem to agree, I get to choose which I tell you first. Brandon, do sit down. It will take a while."

Brandon hesitated, then dropped into the glider beside his uncle.

When he had settled, Becca said, "Good news first. I'm with your uncle—it does make the medicine go down. I got confirmation today, this very morning, that the Georgia Department of Revenue is starting an official investigation into the billing and collecting practices of Melton, our fine and oh-so-scrupulous tax commissioner. And the investigation will go back several years to cover the time span where you were double-billed, Uncle Jake. Melton's in some mighty hot water."

Uncle Jake let out a whoop. "Now if that don't prove what I always say, what goes around comes around! Becca, if you weren't a married woman—and to that big, strappin' Ryan MacIntosh—I'd kiss you!"

She grinned. "It's like any present, sir— it's the thought that counts."

Brandon barely heard the exchange. Unlike his uncle, he was reserving judgment. It was one thing for the crooked tax commissioner to finally get his comeuppance, but did that help Brandon get his uncle's land back? Becca had, after all, mentioned bad news.

"Okay, so that's the good news," he told her.

"Brandon, that ain't good news, that's great news! I told that sapsucker Melton that he'd be sorry, and I'll bet he's sorry now." Uncle Jake offered up his glass to Becca, who fetched her glass and clinked it against his.

Sobering, she settled back in the swing. "All right, Brandon, I know you're fit to be tied, wanting to know what the bad news is. So here goes."

Brandon bit a knuckle as he waited on her.

She didn't dally around. "First of all, you know how long I've been hot-sticking these guys with the revenue department. Since the sheriff's sale that forced Mee-Maw out of her house. It wasn't until after the second auction, the one where Murphy's creditors liquidated everything and I was able to buy back Mee-Maw's farm—"

"And Penelope was able to outbid me for Uncle Jake's," Brandon interjected.

"Yes, and Penelope was able to outbid you, that's right." Becca nodded. "At that point, I finally got hold of someone who would actually listen to me. Today, when I talked with him and he told me about the investigation, he said that if the state was able to prove

Murphy and Melton colluded in order to force Mee-Maw's place into a sheriff's sale, then the sale would be considered null and void. Mee-Maw would get her land back."

"But you bought—"

Becca smiled. "I know. That was my first question, how do I get my money back? My guy at the revenue department said I'd basically have to go back to Murphy's creditors and prove that the land shouldn't have been included in Murphy's assets. With the state voiding the sale, the creditors would be forced to refund me that money."

"But that's great news, Becca!" Brandon leaped to his feet and began to pace. His brain whirred as he tried to figure out what could be so awful in that.

"Yeah. For me."

Brandon turned back to face her at the bleak note in her voice. "But don't you see? This is exactly what I've been trying to explain to Penelope. The land, Uncle Jake's land, should never have been auctioned to begin with, because it was never Murphy's. So the land will go back to Uncle Jake. Penelope can sue to get her money from Murphy's creditors."

"Brandon. I think you'd better sit back down," Becca warned him.

He dropped back into his seat. "What?"

"The reason Mee-Maw can get her land back is that it was originally sold at a sheriff's sale, right? And the state is saying that the county possibly sold it wrongfully, as there was no tax debt to be satisfied. It never should have been sold to begin with."

"Right," Brandon said. "Just like—"

"Your uncle's sale was different. His wasn't a sheriff's sale. It was a private sale. The state's position, even if it is proved that Murphy and Melton colluded and conspired, is that the state didn't force Uncle Jake to sell to Murphy."

Brandon gaped in disbelief. "It sure was a forced sale! If he hadn't sold half his farm to Murphy, the county would have taken his entire place. That's the only reason he did agree to it. He would have never sold if he hadn't been facing a sheriff's sale!"

Becca looked miserable. "I know. I've begged and pleaded, but the state says their hands are tied." She leaned forward and took Uncle Jake's hand in hers. "I'm sorry, sir. It just doesn't seem right that I'll get my money back, eventually anyway, and you don't get your land back."

"Tell me that I'm not hearing this right. Tell me that Murphy's not going to win again because he managed to squeeze Uncle Jake into agreeing to a private sale." Brandon waited for Becca's answer, and when she shook her head, he groaned. "They can't do this! They cannot do this!" He was up again, on his feet, pacing.

"I'm sorry, Brandon."

"Is there nothing we can do?"

Becca pursed her lips. "Not much, but you do have a couple of consolation prizes."

Brandon collapsed back into the glider beside his uncle. He pressed the glass of water against his forehead. It did nothing to cool the boiling anger churning away inside him. "So?"

"If the state convicts Melton, the district attorney here could indict Murphy on extortion charges," Becca told him.

"Right." Brandon kicked at a pebble at his

feet. "Like our sorry D.A. is going to go to the trouble of presenting a grand jury with extortion charges on a guy who's facing a federal indictment. That'll happen when pigs fly."

"Now, hold on, Brandon." Uncle Jake patted Brandon's arm. "She said we had a couple of options."

"The other possibility is that, if Melton gets convicted, you guys could sue Murphy in civil court. A jury might agree with you that it was Murphy's conspiracy with Melton that netted him the land at such a cheap price." Becca shrugged. "Not a great option, but it could be done."

Brandon considered it. "Murphy wouldn't have to be convicted as well?" he asked. "Because you know the D.A.'s not going to bother with indicting him on state charges as long as the feds are interested in Murphy. And for all my complaining, I can see his point. It's not worth the cost to the taxpayers if Murphy's going to be locked up anyway, even if it is some country-club federal prison."

"From what my guy with the state said, no, Murphy wouldn't even have to be indicted,"

Becca said. "As long as the state lays out a strong case—and Melton is convicted—then you can sue for recourse in civil court."

Uncle Jake cleared his throat. "So, okay, Melton gets convicted, put in jail where he belongs, and we go to court and sue Murphy. What happens to Penelope?"

Brandon wheeled around and scrutinized his uncle. He was gratified to see that his uncle really did care about Penelope, but shocked that he himself didn't want Penelope tossed out on her backside.

Maybe it's because you've seen how it hurt Uncle Jake. It wasn't Penelope's fault.

Aloud, though, he theorized, "Well, just like you didn't have to sell it to Murphy—at least, the way the state sees it—Penelope didn't have to buy the land. Maybe the state would see it as caveat emptor."

His uncle waved away Brandon's words. "Becca? What about Penelope?"

"At that point, if they returned the land to you, Uncle Jake," Becca said, "Penelope would have to sue Murphy's creditors to get her money back. But that's a lot more iffy than my situation. For one, the creditors could say they acted in good faith and that Uncle Jake agreed to the land sale. For another, if they did say the land sale was fraudulent, they might limit their liability to Penelope by valuing it at the pre-auction fair-market value. In that case, she wouldn't get all her money back."

Uncle Jake furrowed his brow. "Sounds like a whole lot of cross-your-fingers-and-do-some-serious-hoping mess to me. And I wouldn't want to see that girl suffer because of me. Murphy, now, I'd love to see him with the short end of the stick. But Penelope shouldn't have to pay for her grandfather's sins."

CHAPTER TWENTY

PENELOPE COUNTED back the correct change to Jim Coursey, who took it and the receipt she'd offered.

"Thank you kindly, ma'am," he told her. He bent down to pick up the tractor part she'd welded for him. "That was quick work, and a good price, too."

"You're welcome," she replied. "I'm glad I could help out. Please pass the word to anyone else who needs my services."

Coursey inclined his head. "Yes, ma'am, I surely will."

He turned to go, but Penelope couldn't resist asking, "Who can I thank for referring you to me?"

"Why—" Coursey looked surprised by the question.

Penelope held her breath. She'd had a steady stream of welding customers in the past week. Small jobs, nothing big, but certainly enough to give her hope that she could make it until she sold a project.

She had a growing suspicion that it could only be Brandon.

"I don't mean to put you on the spot." Penelope thought of a reasonable excuse. "I'll give them a twenty-percent discount on the next job they bring me. Same goes for you, too, if you refer me new customers."

"Oh, well, then." Coursey smiled. "I don't guess he'd mind in the slightest. It was Jake Wilkes. He was telling me how you helped him and Brandon when their third link stripped out."

"Oh, okay." Penelope hoped her smile didn't betray her disappointment. "I'll be certain, then, to put Mr. Wilkes down for a discount."

"And I'll pass on the word. Good welding! Shuman had better mind his p's and q's," Coursey said, taking his leave.

Penelope followed him out. She stood in the clearing in front of the open barn doors and stared at the fence.

Brandon had apparently stopped work on tearing it down. She couldn't fathom his reasons. Maybe he'd decided he had been in the wrong. Maybe he'd felt sorry for her. Whatever his motivation, he'd gone back to planting.

And, except for a curt hello, he hadn't spoken to her in the week since.

Sometimes, in the mornings, she'd get up at the first chug of the tractor by her bedroom window, slip into her clothes and stand on the back porch in the predawn darkness. Penelope would let Theo out and drink her coffee, watching as Brandon made the short rows across the field.

He and her mom were right—he spent half his time turning around. It would make more sense to have the fence down.

The strawberry plants were in the ground now, with irrigation pipes running along the black plastic mulching. Penelope recalled the day Brandon and his helper, Prentice, had planted them. She shook her head now as she remembered how little help Brandon had from Prentice.

Prentice at least had spoken to her. He'd wanted to know all about her sculpture, all about the welding she was doing.

Brandon? Tight-lipped, the quintessential man of few words, he'd gone about his business without much more than a nod.

His cool silence had been harder to bear than his previous insults to her grandfather. He seemed to have adopted an indifferent attitude toward her, hard to comprehend after that mind-blowing kiss.

That's what really irritates you, how Brandon can turn it on and turn it off.

Where was that switch, she wondered. Because if Penelope could find it on herself, she'd flip it off.

She'd been awake at five o'clock, waiting to hear his tractor.

It hadn't come.

Sighing, she turned back to the shop and the jobs that waited for her. If she hurried, she could get them all done and work the rest of the day on her sculpture.

No point dreaming away the day on a man who can't forget who you are.

BRANDON RUBBED his temples and frowned down at the inmate report. He liked the money being chief deputy brought him, but

he could do without the paperwork. And the
headaches. This week, the first time back on
days in a while, had proved especially claus-
trophobic.

Or maybe you miss seeing Penelope.

Of course he didn't miss Penelope. He
hadn't spoken to her, right? He'd seen her
on the back porch in the mornings when he'd
set to work on her field—Uncle Jake's field,
not hers. He couldn't help noticing her. She
was like a wounded dog that lurked in the
brush at a distance.

In the week since the fence snafu, he'd
tried to make amends in his own way. He'd
stopped with the fence. He'd sent her business, but he'd told his friends to say Uncle
Jake had sent them. No point giving the
wrong message.

The phone on his desk buzzed, and he
picked it up, thankful for the distraction.

"Deputy Wilkes, how may I help you?"
he asked.

"Is this *Brandon* Wilkes?" The woman's
voice was Yankee, but the inflections were
Southern enough. And the voice seemed
vaguely familiar to him.

"Yes, ma'am, it is. How may I help you?"

"Well." An embarrassed laugh punctuated the moment of silence. "I'm Marlene Langston."

His stomach lifted, then settled back. "Oh. You're, uh, Penelope Langston's mother, then."

"That's right, that's exactly right. I had some paperwork that Penelope wanted me to do for her and I needed to fax it to you."

"Paperwork?" Suspicious, he stopped doodling on the legal pad he kept by the phone.

"Yes, the rental agreement. Penelope said she'd never bothered to get one done, and I thought I'd take care of it for her."

"Well...we had a verbal agreement."

"I know, I know, Penelope said as much. I need to finish up some details. I understand you are renting the land for...how much an acre?"

"She hadn't named a price." Now that he had the field planted, Penelope was intent on squeezing out every nickel she could.

"What exactly did she say?"

"That I could use the land. She said she wasn't using it."

A laugh that sounded so much like Penelope's came across the line. "That's my daughter for you. Absolutely no business sense. But okay, I'll put it in the agreement that the only recompense she'll get is for you to replace the fence when you're done."

"I beg your pardon?" Brandon dropped the pencil on the desk and fumbled to get it back.

"The fence. You took it down so that you could plow?"

"But I haven't. Penelope said—" Brandon broke off.

"She said what?"

"Don't you two talk? I mean, haven't you discussed this if you're preparing her rental agreement?"

"Well, truth be told—" Marlene laughed again, "—Penelope's hard to reach sometimes. She gets caught up in her latest project…well, you know."

Brandon didn't know, but there was no point in saying so. He waited out the silence and was rewarded by Marlene clearing her throat.

"Ahem, yes, so the latest information I have is that the fence can come down as long as you agree to put it back up when the agreement expires. Is that okay with you?"

Brandon couldn't answer. If he said yes, his long-range backup plan of getting the land back through adverse possession was toast. If he didn't…

She's meeting you more than halfway. Don't be a jerk about it…. Yeah, she can afford to be generous. Possession is nine-tenths of the law.

But Marlene had moved on. "I'll fax over the agreement and anything you and Penelope have discussed, you can add as an addendum, how about it?"

"Okay. That sounds…okay. Honestly, Penelope seemed to feel strongly about the fence. I'd want to talk to her about it before I signed it."

"Yes, yes, of course. Now, there's another little matter."

Man, he could tell Marlene was Southern, despite her Yankee accent. She could beat around the bush like nobody's business. The way she said "little matter" signaled to Brandon there was nothing little about it.

"Yes?" he prompted when she didn't elaborate.

"This is embarrassing. But I understand you don't particularly care for my father."

"Richard Murphy? That's a polite way of putting it. No offense, ma'am."

"None taken. My father is a difficult man at his best. But he can be very charming. And that's why I'm so concerned about Penelope."

"She's a big girl. She can take care of herself."

Marlene's uneasy chuckle told him she didn't agree. What had Penelope said? Something about her parents not taking her no for an answer? He could see that about Marlene.

"Would you say that the federal indictment against him is an inevitability? It's certainly taking a long time if it is."

Brandon glanced back at the reports still waiting to be filled out and tried not to grind his teeth. "The feds are thorough, and the U.S. attorneys are protective of their conviction rate. So they don't move forward with an indictment unless and until they believe they have an airtight case. If you get a federal indictment handed down against you, it's a fair assurance you'll be convicted. It's almost a one-way ticket to the federal pen."

He heard a clicking noise, as though Marlene was tapping a pen against her teeth. "I see. Did he do it? This farm scam? Is he guilty?"

"Up to his neck in it, ma'am. I'm sure sorry to tell you that, but it's the truth. He's been defrauding federal crop insurance programs for years on a smaller scale, but this past year, he moved up to a new level and he involved a lot of farmers in the area. He wanted my best friend to get involved, and when Ryan wouldn't, he conspired with the tax commissioner to force a property sale."

Marlene hissed. "That would be that horrid Melton, wouldn't it? The man is a crook. How he keeps getting elected is beyond me."

"You remember your Brazelton County history, then, I guess. But Melton's not smart enough to have come up with this on his own."

"No, leave it to my father to dream that up."

"Ma'am, if you don't mind me asking, why is it that you hate your father so much, yet

Penelope is one of his biggest champions? Doesn't she know what kind of person he is?"

Marlene sighed. "That's to my unending regret. I tried, you know, to do the right thing. I wanted to be fair. I wanted her to be able to grow up and see him as he was, without my...prejudices getting in her way. She knows I don't get along well with him. I suppose, though, that she discounts it as fallout from my parents' divorce."

"It's not just that?" Reports could wait, Marlene might have some information he could use. He poised the pencil over the legal pad.

"Not exactly. There were things my father did, things I'm ashamed of. I didn't know about them at the time, or at least I didn't understand them, but later they were...illuminating. I never could view him in quite the same light."

"And Penelope knows whatever it is he did?"

"Oh, no. Like I said, I was trying to be fair."

"Well," Brandon said drily, "looks as though that went well."

"I had no idea he'd talk her into buying a piece of property that close to him! I thought I'd die of shock when she told me. I tried so hard to talk her out of it, but once Penelope gets her mind set, there's no changing it."

"So Murphy contacted her then?"

"Oh, yes. He actually tried his luck with Trent first, but Trent didn't buy his con for a minute."

"Why exactly are you telling me all this? What do you think I can do?"

Again her laugh told Brandon that Marlene was clearly embarrassed. "Well, you know, he calls me from time to time, my father does. And he seems quite concerned about your influence over Penelope."

"My influence over Penelope? That would be zip."

"No, no, I don't think so. One thing my father could always do was spot a potential weak link in any plan he was putting together. He tried to convince me that you meant to harm Penelope. So I figure, if he's up to his old tricks, you're the person who could come closest to helping her."

"Don't mind me for saying so, ma'am, but that's a big leap."

"Yes, I'm aware of that. But Penelope seems to like you when you're not— Anyway, to get to the point, one of my points, of this call, I was wondering if you had any vacation time coming up."

Brandon tried to follow the conversation's change in direction but couldn't. "Ma'am?"

"Vacation time. Personal leave?"

"I have some built up, but why do you ask?"

"My son—I mentioned Trent a moment ago—is getting married. In a week. And I was wondering…"

"Uh-huh?" Brandon held his breath. He had an inkling what was coming and wasn't sure what his answer would be.

"If I bought your ticket, could you fly out with Penelope? To attend the wedding."

"To Oregon?"

"Yes. It wouldn't be for long. The wedding is on a Saturday, so you'd fly in late Thursday and fly out Sunday morning."

"Uh, ma'am, I appreciate the offer, but I'm not real keen on flying."

"You see," she said, as if he hadn't spoken. "I've tried so hard to convince Penelope that there's no good in helping out her grandfather. She won't listen, and I'm terribly afraid she's about to do something she'll come to regret."

Brandon groaned. He had no interest at all in getting in the middle of an old family quarrel. He started to protest, again, that Penelope was old enough to make her own mistakes. "Perhaps you—"

But Marlene steamrolled on. "I'd like to talk to you, show you some things to do with my father that perhaps should go to the authorities investigating him? But before I did that, I'd want to meet you. In person. Can you understand that?" she pleaded. "This is a big thing I'm doing, a momentous decision. And I haven't…it's hard, bringing my family's dirty laundry out in the open. I need to know what sort of person you are before I share some very painful things with you. So can you come?"

CHAPTER TWENTY-ONE

"YOU DID *what?*" Penelope's near-shriek sent Theo skittering toward the hall. "Mom, how could you? How could you invite that man to Trent's wedding?"

"It seemed like a perfectly good idea. I did warn you that you'd need a date. After all, it's a long flight, and who better than your friend from Georgia to keep you company?"

Penelope seethed at her mother's mild-mannered answer. The innocence reeked of conspiracy. This was the same attitude Mom had had when she'd arranged with Penelope's landlord—landlords, plural, because it had happened more than once—to inspect her fridge for food. *Well, dear, they were on the way to the market themselves, and I thought...*

"Mom, he's not my friend." Penelope stared down at the e-ticket in her hand and closed her eyes at the sight of Brandon's name. "Didn't I tell you he was trying to take down the fence between our properties? A friend does not do that."

"Oh, pish-posh, Penelope! He was simply tired of driving that tractor on the open road. He seems like a very nice fellow. You should give him a chance. You're not getting any younger, you know."

"Is this a matchmaking trip?" Now Penelope really lost it. "Mom, I swear—"

"Honestly. What is the problem? I get to invite who I want to invite. And I've decided Brandon is as good as anybody. Why do you object? Is he horribly disfigured in some way?"

"No," she admitted. "The opposite in fact. He's…" Her mind's eye traveled over Brandon's dark eyes, his chiseled features and broad shoulders.

"He's what?"

"He's good-looking. Enough. I guess. If you, uh, like them that way. But it's not that. Even if he were, how'd you put it, horribly disfigured, that wouldn't matter to me. You know that."

"But he is nice. I had quite a long chat with him on the phone, and I thought, why not?"

Penelope rubbed her forehead. Why was it that every time she talked to her mother on the phone, she got a headache? She ought to invest in Excedrin stock. "I don't get this. You won't have Grandpa Murphy at the wedding, but you invite the man who hates him? The one who's trying to put Grandpa in jail? And is conspiring to take my property? Mom!"

"Perhaps your grandfather needs no help whatsoever finding his way to jail. Have you thought about that, Penelope? Hmm?"

"He's your father. I don't care what sort of bad blood is between you two, you can't want your own father in prison."

Marlene sighed. "Of course I don't. But he's an adult, and he's made his bed. As for you, I don't see what the problem is about having Brandon along."

She never would, Penelope realized. She would never in a million years understand how awkward a transcontinental flight would be with someone you couldn't talk to for more than two minutes without either arguing or…

Say it, Penelope. Kissing like nobody's business.

"Grandpa's just going to be that much more hurt."

"I'm sorry about that. But your grandfather is well aware of the reasons that I no longer consider him part of my family, and it's none of your concern." That's how her mother had always ended any conversation about Grandpa Murphy. "Now are you going to be the adult you say you are and give Brandon the ticket information, or am I going to have to send that to him?"

"Oh, all right," Penelope said, dispensing with any attempt at graciousness in defeat. "I hope you're happy."

"But I am, darling. Supremely. See you soon!"

PENELOPE BLEW out a breath and stared first at the e-ticket and then at the front of the sheriff's department. Might as well get this over with, because it surely wasn't something to linger over.

At the front door of the building, she saw someone coming out and she stopped to let him by.

"Oh, Penelope. Hey! You made the people yet?" Prentice asked. "I sure want to see 'em. They'll look funny all shiny. You sure you're not gonna paint 'em? You know, so they look real? Cause, you know, they might look like…" Here he dropped his voice and cast his eyes first one way and then the other. "You know. Aliens."

Penelope couldn't help smiling. The day Prentice had helped Brandon with the strawberries, he hadn't understood that there would be no actual figure of a man or woman in her sculpture. It appeared as though he still hadn't quite grasped the concept. "Uh, no, Prentice. I won't be painting them. But I promise, they won't look like aliens."

"Good! 'Cause you never know. Those aliens could think you were inviting 'em on in."

"I'll keep that in mind, Prentice."

"You looking for Brandon? He's in there. Grouchy, though. Says he's busy. If he'd let me have a patrol car and a gun, I could help him. I sure could. I'm a real deputy, you know. Brandon gave me a star." He tapped the toy badge on his chest.

Penelope's bad mood evaporated in the presence of Prentice's earnestness. "I'll bet you could help Brandon out. But I'm sure you do already, in lots of ways, like you did with those strawberries."

"Yum. They gonna be yummy, aren't they, Penelope? When spring comes?"

"Uh, yeah." Penelope's mood took a hit when she thought about all those strawberry pickers descending on her. Oh, well. Maybe she could get the first crop. A strawberry pie fresh from the field might prove tasty.

Behind Prentice, Penelope saw movement as Brandon came out. "Prentice, don't you be—" He stopped when he saw Penelope.

"Uh, hi. Is Geraldine out again?"

"No. I have something my mother wanted me to give you, actually."

"Your mother?"

"Yes. Apparently you've signed on to be my escort for my brother's wedding. I have your plane ticket."

Prentice spoke up. "But Brandon, you hate flying. You hate planes. Remember? You swore you'd never fly again."

Penelope did note a certain greenish tinge to Brandon's face at the mention of plane tickets. Her heart softened. Perhaps this whole thing was more of her mother's trademark won't-take-no-for-an-answer.

"Prentice, could I catch you later? I need to talk to Penelope."

"Are you really going somewhere with Penelope? Where? On a plane? I'll go if you don't want to go, Brandon. I love flying! Remember, I told you about me and my sister going to Washington D.C.? We flew, on an actual *airplane*. And it was stormy! And the lightning was so close."

Brandon's face went that much greener. "Penelope, why don't you come in my office? Prentice, I'll see you around, okay? Don't you be hunting any more aliens, now, not without me around. That's a direct order from the sheriff."

Prentice looked downcast but he nodded. "Oh, okay. But I swear, if you'd seen that thing, you would have thought it was a miniature spaceship, too." He turned and shuffled down the steps.

Brandon sighed and waved a hand inside. As Penelope brushed past him, she heard him mutter, "I just don't have enough imagination to keep him out of trouble."

"Imagination?"

"Yeah." He looked sheepish. "I can't imagine enough things he can get into so I can order him not to get into it. If you tell him not to do something, then he listens. But I can't think of everything."

Inside his tiny office, Brandon pulled up a folding chair for her. "A corner office it's not, but *mi casa es su casa.*"

"Thanks." She sat down as Brandon leaned against the corner of his desk, then she stood back up. "I'm sure you have loads to get done, so I won't keep you. It's just this—" She fluttered a piece of paper in his direction. "The confirmation slip for the e-ticket. To fly out for Trent's wedding."

Brandon went green on her again. He didn't take the paper from her. "That. Prentice was right, flying doesn't really agree with me. I can't think why I said yes to your mother. I should have realized that when you, uh, go to Oregon, you've got to fly. Ha-ha."

"You don't have to go, you know. My mom can be fairly hard to say no to. I speak from experience."

"You don't want me to go?"

Penelope groaned inwardly. "I don't care one way or the other." She slid her fingers behind her back and crossed them. "I didn't want you to get roped into something you didn't want to do."

Brandon shrugged. "Hey, why not? She's offering, and where else will I get a vacation with the plane ticket and the free accommodations?"

"Free accommodations?" Penelope's smile faltered.

"Yeah, well, if I survive the plane trip, your mom's putting me up in one of her guest rooms."

Good grief. "Really. Mom failed to mention that. But that's just like Mom!" Penelope said brightly.

"You sure you don't mind?"

"Actually, I feel sorry for you. I know what it's like to get in Mom's path. You have that look."

"Oh. Well, she was persuasive. But on the plus side, it's a chance to see the Pacific, right? I've never been to the West Coast."

"Bend is in central Oregon, actually. The

coast is over the mountains, and depending on the weather—"

"Oh." Brandon looked so disappointed that suddenly Penelope wanted to be sure he saw the Pacific—and that she was the one who showed it to him.

"I tell you what, I'll see if I can't get an earlier flight out. If it's not going to cost the earth to change it, we'll fly into Portland on Wednesday instead of Redmond on Thursday. That way, maybe we can see the ocean."

Brandon smiled, that same smile he'd given her when she'd offered to fix the broken link on his plow. "You'd do that?"

"Yeah. Sure. I love the ocean. We can drive to my grandmother's house and over to Cape Meares State Park—that's on the ocean. Walk on the beach, maybe see some sea lions?"

"Okay. Now if I can find my way to be brave enough to get on that plane."

"Nothing to it," she assured him. "I'll hold your hand the whole way."

Brandon's eyes darkened with an emotion she couldn't read and the air between them crackled. Penelope's mouth went dry, and she ran a tongue over equally dry lips, preparing to say anything to break the tension.

"Don't," he said, grasping her hand.

"Don't what?"

He pulled her up against him. "I'll regret this," he whispered, then bent his head to kiss her.

The paper in her hands crumpled against his chest as she leaned into the kiss, but she paid no mind to it. Instead, she concentrated on the way he held her close, the way his lips felt on hers, the way their breaths mingled.

When he stepped back, it was Penelope who whispered, "Don't. Don't go all cold on me." And before he could, she flung the crumpled confirmation slip onto his desk and bolted from the room.

CHAPTER TWENTY-TWO

THE DAY OF Penelope and Brandon's departure dawned clear and bright and unseasonably warm, even for Georgia. She dreaded the twenty-degree cooler weather she'd find in Oregon, and the rain that would greet them at Portland.

But first she had to make the flight out from Savannah, and Theo had conspired to make that almost impossible. For once in his feline life, he'd not served as her alarm clock and she'd overslept. Then he'd managed to trip her up every time she'd gone from closet to overnight bag to throw things in.

"Honestly, Theo. I'd take you if I could, but you hate flying." She bumped him off her dark wool pants and cringed at the amount of white cat hair on them. "Note to self—next time, no flame-point Siamese—white fur shows up on everything."

Apparently insulted, Theo jumped off the

bed and stalked toward his food bowl in the kitchen. Penelope sighed over the pants and stuck a sticky pet-hair roller in the corner of her already crammed suitcase.

An insistent banging on the back door sent Theo skittering back in her room to cower under the bed.

"Brandon?" Penelope shouted. "I'm almost ready—hold on!" She struggled with the zipper of the bag and couldn't do it up.

The banging started again, louder. "Aaargh!" she growled, finally putting a knee on the bag in a vain effort to get it to zip. The zipper started enthusiastically enough, but stuck about halfway around.

The knocking had ceased. She unzipped the bag, scooted some things around and glared at her space hog of a hair dryer. No way was she going to be reduced to borrowing someone else's at her parents. Something else would have to go before it.

Now the banging came from the front porch, louder even than before.

"Brandon, I said I was coming!" she shouted, but it didn't stop the banging. She yanked so hard on the zipper that the tassel broke off and she stumbled backward.

"Oh, all right, then." Penelope gave up on the bag and stomped up the hallway. "Brandon Wilkes!" she ground out as she flung open the door. "Did you not hear—"

But it wasn't Brandon.

It was Grandpa Murphy.

Her stomach took a guilty dive downward. "Grandpa," she said. "I didn't know it was you."

"I gathered that," Grandpa Murphy said icily as he pushed past her. "And the door was locked. What's that about?"

"Well, uh, I wanted to keep people from simply walking in, that's all. Is something wrong?"

"Like my lawyers hounding me for money? Or the feds calling me in, telling me I could make it easy on myself by cutting a deal? Yeah, my whole life's in the toilet." He studied her. "You look mighty dressed up. Where are you off to?"

Penelope bit her lip. "I have to fly back home to Oregon today, Grandpa. I was finishing my packing when I heard you at the door."

"Home? Home's here! Why you got to leave me now? You're leaving today? Why didn't you tell me about it?"

Because I couldn't figure out a way to tell you that you weren't invited to your own grandson's wedding.

"I've been busy, I guess, and you haven't been coming by." How could she ease him out the door before Brandon showed up? The one thing she didn't need was to have the two of them at each other's throats. That would make for a pleasant plane trip, she thought sourly, and a bad note to leave her grandfather on.

"So what's this about Brandon Wilkes?" Instead of taking any hint to leave, Grandpa Murphy headed up the hallway toward the kitchen. "You got any coffee on? I don't smell any coffee. Honey, I've told you Wilkes is bad news. You know he is if he's trying to railroad me into this federal indictment."

The one thing I cannot figure out about Brandon, the one thing that makes absolutely no sense. Why would he do that to an inno-cent old man?

"Grandpa, I'm really on my way out the door. I didn't even have time to make a pot of coffee this morning." She trailed him up the hall, glancing longingly at her suitcase through the open bedroom door. Theo peeked out from under the bed, his ears laid back flat. He hissed at the strange feet tramping through the house.

"You just go on ahead. Don't mind me. I'll get by on my own. Say, how long you gonna be gone? 'Cause Todd and Rudy want a sit-down with you. That's why I came by. Hadn't done me a bit of good to call you. You never answer that phone of yours."

Penelope was glad Grandpa Murphy didn't turn to see her face. She was sure guilt leaked from every pore. She had been ducking his calls, because she didn't want to have to tell him about Trent's wedding.

"Todd and Rudy?" The names confused her. "Who are Todd and Rudy?"

He paused as he yanked out a dinette chair. "The solid-waste guys, the guys from Flor-ida. Haven't you been listening to a thing I tell you? They want to meet you and get this land deal settled."

Penelope stifled a groan. Not the landfill again. "Grandpa, I hope you haven't been leading these men on about this land. I'm not sure I want to sell it. Not to them, anyway."

"Why not?" His eyebrows lowered in a thunderous frown. "I need the money, Penelope. My lawyers are threatening to cut me off if I don't get them some and soon. And you could get it for me with this land deal. You said you'd meet with these guys."

"I did, didn't I?" Why on earth had she ever agreed? "Well, you're going to have to put them off. We're not flying back into Savannah until Sunday evening."

He shot her a suspicious glance as he settled into the chair. "We? Who's we?"

"Uh—" Her self-flagellation at her slip was interrupted by the rumble of a truck. That would be Brandon. Penelope closed her eyes and rubbed them.

I'll pay now, she thought.

Sure enough, Grandpa Murphy came out of his seat like a rocket when he spied Brandon's truck through the kitchen window. "What on earth—" He spun on Penelope. "You tell me, and tell me now, that boy isn't the one going with you to Oregon."

Penelope peeked at her grandfather through her fingers. "Uh…I can't."

"Why not?"

"Because it wouldn't be true?" She cringed and dropped her hand. "Listen, it's not what you're thinking."

"I don't know what to think, you hauling off across the country with a man who wants to see me come out of prison in a pine box. Penny, you know if I go to jail, at my age, I ain't coming out. You know that! You gotta know that."

"Grandpa, calm down. Look, you're upset about the lawyers."

"Sure I'm upset and I've got every reason to be upset. They're sucking my soul dry, while you're off having the time of your life with the man who's the reason I need the soul-suckers in the first place!" Grandpa's face had turned purple and his chest heaved.

"Wait. This isn't my idea. You have to believe me."

"Not your idea. Well, if it's not your idea,

then you tell him to stay right here! Are you? Or are you gonna betray me, Penny? What's it gonna be? Can I count on you? Or are you gonna turn out like your mother after all?"

BRANDON GROANED as he recognized Murphy's truck. The man was like a bad penny. It was as if he had a radar locked on Brandon.

Brandon threw the truck into Park and fumed for a moment. He was of half a mind to forget the trip and go home.

But the temptation to find dirt on Murphy called out to him. Marlene Langston had made it crystal clear: either Brandon came and presented himself for inspection, or he didn't get to see the family skeletons.

He'd got little sleep the night before—or all this week. The impulsive kiss he'd given Penelope, not to mention her last whispered plea for him not to go cold on her, had tormented him. Why couldn't he keep his hands off her?

Murphy's truck in Penelope's yard was reason enough for Brandon to never touch her again. But would he be able to keep his head when he was all the way across the country, away from things like this to remind him of why she was all wrong for him?

Now or never, Brandon decided. If they didn't leave soon, they'd miss their flight out. Uncle Jake had offered to drive them to Savannah, and he drove slow.

Brandon heaved himself out of the truck and made his way up the back porch steps. He hesitated when he heard Murphy's raised voice. Through the window he could see Penelope's features twisted with emotion, and she was gripping the back of her dinette chair so hard her knuckles were white.

Enough of this garbage.

Brandon rapped on the back door. Penelope snapped her head around in his direction. Slowly, she waved him in.

The room was oppressively silent when he stepped inside. "Penelope? Are you ready?"

"Almost," she said with a brightness he could tell was false because it contradicted the panic in her eyes.

"So, where's your suitcase? Uncle Jake's waiting for us back at his house. I'm letting him drive my truck."

"Uh, you know, I haven't finished zipping it. Stubborn zippers!" Penelope's laugh seemed forced. "Do you mind? It's in the bedroom, second door on the left."

"Not a problem." He ducked his head in curt acknowledgment to Murphy. "I'll let you two say your goodbyes."

In the bedroom, he spotted a hugely obese overnight bag on the bed. As he shoved down on the bag's lid to manage the zipper, Theo came out from under the bed just long enough to startle Brandon, wind around his ankles and scoot back under.

"Oh, so we're friends now?" Brandon asked in a low voice. "You took to heart that business about Murphy not having any animals he couldn't eat? Uncle Jake's the one you'd better be nice to. He's feeding you." The zipper slid home and Brandon set the bag on the floor.

Hushed voices floated down the hallway, but Brandon couldn't make out what was being said. He waited another minute or so in the hopes that Murphy would leave before he went back into the kitchen.

Theo came back out for another guerrilla rub on the ankles, and this time Brandon risked reaching down to stroke the cat on the back. "Glad you're seeing things my way, finally. You reckon you could talk to your mistress?"

The cat's purr sounded like an engine with a bad knock. Then as abruptly as Theo had come out, he ducked back under the bed. Brandon glanced at his watch. No more time to wait around, and Murphy hadn't budged.

Brandon hefted the bag. The low voices didn't get any clearer as he approached the kitchen door, just got lower and more intense. When he crossed the threshold, Penelope cast an anxious smile his way.

Taking in Murphy's glower, Brandon set his jaw. This time, he would not lose his temper. The sorry excuse for humanity wasn't worth it. "Are you ready, Penelope?" he asked. "We're cutting it close."

"Oh, good, you got my suitcase zipped." Again Penelope exuded a false brightness. "Let me pet my cat and we'll be out of here. Grandpa, I'll talk more about this on Sunday when I get in, okay?"

Murphy didn't take the hint. He remained in the chair, stolid and sour.

Penelope gave it another go. "I wish we had more time to discuss this, but I really do have to go."

Murphy narrowed his eyes. "Well, go on, then. I'm sure not stopping you. Go on and leave me."

Penelope rubbed her eyes. "I need to lock up, Grandpa."

Brandon saw Murphy's right fingers drum out a near-silent tattoo on the dinette table, and he knew, in an instant, that Murphy was waiting her out. The old buzzard wanted her to leave him in the house. It was some sort of power play.

"I'll lock 'em. When I leave. I'm just going to sit here for a while. Maybe make some of that good coffee of yours, Penny-girl."

Now Penelope's face betrayed her displeasure. "No, Grandpa, let's all leave together. I need to lock up. I'll worry about it, you know?"

"Can't you trust me?" Murphy asked her in a low voice.

Just say it, Penelope. Say you don't want him in your house. Tell him no, and mean it.

"Sure, I trust you, Grandpa." Penelope gestured to the back door with her hand. "But I'll follow you out."

"You're gonna turn an old man out? When all he wants is a chance to get his breath back and drink a cup of coffee? Are you serious? You think I'm going to steal some of your stuff? Ha! You're worrying about the wrong guy. That one you're hauling off to Oregon with, now, he's the one you need to worry about."

Brandon clamped his fingers in a death grip on Penelope's bag and wished it was Murphy's neck instead. Still he said nothing, just clenched his teeth shut so no words could escape.

"Grandpa. I have to leave now. And you know I'm going to miss my flight if I don't go. So could you please leave?"

Murphy looked from Penelope to Brandon, and Brandon could swear he saw him calculating behind those eyes.

"No. I got a right to be here."

That was Brandon's breaking point. He dropped the bag and crossed to Murphy. "Listen, you—you—" He bit off the words he wanted to use. "She's asked you to leave, a lot nicer than I would have. She wants you out of here. Now. So it's either you leave on your own free will or I call in another deputy, and he'll take you off my hands. I won't lie. It'd be my pleasure to put you in a patrol car myself, even if I did miss my flight."

CHAPTER TWENTY-THREE

PENELOPE SEETHED as she sat between Uncle Jake on her left and Brandon on her right. Her thoughts raced.

Why did Grandpa put me in that position?

Didn't Brandon think me capable of showing my own grandfather out?

If it were anyone but Brandon, Grandpa wouldn't...

Brandon, for his part, let a smug smile play at the corners of his mouth. He was happy, *happy* that he'd strong-armed an old man.

If Grandpa had left when you asked him...

Uncle Jake interrupted the silence and Penelope's tumultuous thoughts. "Got something I want to show y'all."

"We're running out of time, Uncle Jake," Brandon pointed out, "especially with you driving."

"Won't take a minute, and it's on the way. And then, if you're in such an all-fired-up hurry, I'll swap with you and you can risk body and bone. Besides, this way is almost a shortcut to the interstate."

Five minutes later, the truck bumped down a washboard dirt road. Uncle Jake pulled to a stop at a grove of pine trees. He opened the truck door. "Well, c'mon. Y'all are in a hurry, right?"

Muttering under his breath, Brandon slid out and offered Penelope a hand. She wasn't sure she wanted it. She wasn't sure she ever wanted him to touch her again.

But she took the hand he offered and maneuvered her way to the ground.

"Watch that hole," he warned and, instead of letting go, guided her around it. The contact of his skin on hers reminded her too much of their kiss. But the easy, impersonal way he let her go once the hole was negotiated hurt more.

Rounding the truck, Brandon asked, "What's so important for us to see?"

"This here," Uncle Jake answered. He pointed his sun-spotted hand at an old tractor, with strange metal wheels, stuck between two pine trees.

"Uncle Jake! We could have seen this any-time. I've seen it before," Brandon protested.

"Ah, but you need to hear about it."

Penelope succumbed to curiosity. "This tractor's been here a while if two pines grew up on either side of it. That's what happened? Someone abandoned the tractor and the pine trees grew up around it?"

"Exactly!" Jake beamed his approval, much like a teacher to a prize student. "See, this ol' thing's flywheel got busted. Farmer who owned it didn't have the time or the money to fix it, so he just wound up kicking the tar out of it, which helped his frustration a smidge, but that's 'bout all."

Uncle Jake walked over and slid a hand along the hood of the tractor. "He could have asked his neighbors to help. But his pride got in the way, like pride is wont to do. And so first one thing and another happened. Life had a way of getting away from him, and when he finally came back to fix the tractor, these trees had grown up."

"What did he use for a tractor?" Penelope asked. The surreal arrangement of antique tractor and two pines on either side of the driver's seat appealed to the sculptor in her.

"Not important." Uncle Jake waved away the question. "The important thing is—why didn't he cut the trees down?"

She met Brandon's gaze and saw the same aha-why-didn't-I-think-of-that in his eyes that she was feeling.

"I give up. Why not?"

"Simple." Now Uncle Jake patted one of the trees. "These pine trees were just doing what pine trees do—growing up. And the man realized that it was all his fault anyway. Instead of kicking the tires on the tractor, he could have dispensed with his pride and asked his neighbors for a hand. Why cut down two pine trees that didn't mean no harm? So here it sits, this monument to human stubbornness and to how a problem ignored just gets worse. You leave something to be fixed later, and you'll come back to see it stuck between two pine trees."

Penelope instantly got Uncle Jake's meaning, and from Brandon's glum expression, she could tell he did as well. Her earlier anger dissipated. "You're a regular Aesop, Uncle Jake."

"I been told that." He hitched up his overalls with more than a glimmer of pride. "Now that I've said my piece, let's get y'all to that airport."

UNCLE JAKE'S PARABLE had left Brandon silent all the way down to Savannah. Penelope had attempted to draw Brandon out a couple of times, but he'd answered her questions with a distracted yes or no. Then he'd gone back to staring out at the miles of pine trees blipping by on I-16.

When Uncle Jake had hefted her carry-on bag out from behind the truck seat, he looked as though he was going to say something to Brandon. Penelope waited, but in the end, Uncle Jake just shook Brandon's hand, gave her a hug and bade the two of them goodbye and good luck.

They spent another near-silent forty-five minutes waiting on their flight to Atlanta. Brandon had bought them some lunch at a fast-food place, but beyond "Need some ketchup?" or "Can I get that straw for you?" he didn't say much of anything.

It unnerved Penelope. Was this the way it was going to be the whole time?

On the airplane, he tightened his seat belt, checked it again and then glanced around. She saw more than a little panic in his expression.

"Hey." Penelope slid her fingers through his. "Remember? Hand-holding therapy?"

Brandon squeezed her hand in response with fingers damp with sweat. "I told you I hate flying. I cannot imagine what possessed me to get on this plane."

"It will be okay," she assured him, deciding that now would not be the time to remind him he had at least two more plane changes ahead of him.

The plane began meandering down the taxiway, then made the turn and started gathering speed for takeoff. Brandon shut his eyes tightly.

"It's worse if you have your eyes closed," she whispered. "Just look at me."

And he did. Though his hand was still damp and his jaw was clenched tight, he gave Penelope a level stare. She smiled at him, and he returned a green-around-the-gills grin. The plane grabbed at air, bounced with turbulence that Penelope would never have noticed if Brandon hadn't been so nervous beside her. His gaze darted around wildly.

Penelope reached up and touched a finger to his chin. It brought his attention back to her. "Hey, trust me," she whispered. "The worst part's almost over."

"Uh, if you say so."

Then the ascent smoothed out, though the climb was still steep. Brandon's breathing eased and his death grip on her hand slackened.

"Feel better?" she asked.

"Amazingly enough, I do."

"Good!" Impulsively she pressed a kiss to his jaw, which made him jump.

"I'm sorry." Penelope drew back.

But he held on to her hand and laid his other one on top of hers. "No. It's fine. It surprised me, that's all. I'm a nervous wreck from this flying business. I must have completely missed out on Uncle Jake's genes."

"His genes? I don't understand."

"You didn't know? He flew a fighter plane in World War II, loved flying. He was offered a job flying for an airline when he came home. But he loved farming even more than flying."

He frowned and stared down at his knees, which were jammed into the tight space coach afforded them. Penelope patted the knee closest to her with her free hand. "I like your uncle. He's unexpected, in a lot of ways. That country-bumpkin act is a mask, isn't it? His send-off was much better than my grandfather's. I'm sorry you felt you had to get involved."

He raised his gaze back up to meet hers. "I suppose I should apologize. Murphy didn't look as though he was going to listen to you. It made me mad, him not respecting you enough to—"

Whatever he would have said, he didn't finish. Brandon abruptly said, "Let's forget it all. The land, Murphy, the fence, every bad word you and I have ever said to each other. For this trip. Let's just have a good time."

She waited for him to explain the sudden

truce he offered. When he didn't, she nodded and smiled. "Sounds good to me."

THEY LANDED in Portland in a steady downpour that Penelope had trouble negotiating in her economy rental car. The headlights illuminated a dark city just saying goodbye to another fall day of rain. Penelope missed the sunshine and blue skies she'd left behind in Georgia.

"So we're, what, driving over to the coast tonight?" Brandon asked.

"Yeah, it's still—how do you Georgia boys put it? A ways away?" She cast him a quick smile. "Like I said, I couldn't get us a later flight out tomorrow, so I decided we do this now. I wanted you to see the Pacific."

"And how do we get to Bend?" Brandon shifted in the tight confines of the Corolla. "We're driving?"

"No. I was going to, but my worrywart mother thinks we wouldn't get there in time for the rehearsal dinner tomorrow night. Something about bad weather over the mountains. So we'll stay at my grandmother's tonight, then head back here to Portland to catch a flight to Redmond."

"Oh, joy. More planes. If there's supposed to be bad weather, wouldn't we be safer with our feet on the ground?"

Penelope laughed. "Obviously you haven't driven along a mountain pass in bad weather."

"My gut is telling me to avoid any plane if at all possible, but I defer to your judgment. I'd hate to get stuck in a blizzard in the mountains."

"Wouldn't be a blizzard, not this time of year. Well, I guess anything's possible. But still it can be nasty."

Brandon yawned and leaned back against the headrest. The yawn reminded Penelope of how tired she was. "So your grandmother. Is this Murphy's ex-wife?"

She jumped at Brandon's mention of her grandfather and felt a swirling amalgam of guilt and irritation when she recalled how she'd left Grandpa Murphy.

Penelope shook her head. "No, Granny Lou lives near my parents in Bend. You'll see her at the wedding. And actually, Grams— my dad's mom—doesn't live in her house anymore. She's in a retirement home in Bend.

But she still has the house in Tillamook, and we can stay there. If you don't mind."

"Hey, I'm just along for the ride. What's she like, anyway? Do you take after her?"

"You'd like her. She's a lot like Uncle Jake—full of stories that always have a moral. She and my grandfather ran a farm for years, until he passed away. It's beautiful."

"Yeah? She farms? And you didn't inherit her green thumb?" Brandon teased.

"It was a dairy farm. Milk cows, now, I know a little something about. And butter and cheese. But growing stuff beyond my vegetable patch? Nada." She laughed. "A total dunce when it comes to planting for market. I think that's what's so interesting about seeing you farm my land—how you tend it, coax things to life on it. Those strawberries, you've put a lot of work into them."

Brandon was silent. A look his way told her that he was back to staring out the window. What had she said to plunge him back into moodiness?

"It's hard for me to think of it as your land," he said suddenly.

"What?"

"You said, 'seeing you farm my land.' I've always seen it as my uncle's and—maybe, one day in the hopefully very distant future—mine." Brandon turned back to her. "I know, I said no talk about any of that. But it's never far from my mind."

"You're never going to see the loss of it as anything but my grandfather's fault, are you?" Penelope tightened her grip on the wheel.

"No. I'm sorry, Penelope. But no, I'll always blame Murphy."

And then Brandon went back to staring out the window.

CHAPTER TWENTY-FOUR

THE RAIN HAD SLOWED to a drizzle by the time they'd made the long drive across to Tillamook and out to Penelope's grandmother's farm. For the most part, Brandon had feigned sleep as a way to avoid having to talk with her. And to get a chance to think.

Now, as the car slowed, he sat up and peered through the evening's darkness. He could see a gate blocking the driveway and a paint-peeled Langston Dairies sign on the fence beside it.

"Need me to get out and open the gate?" he offered.

He must have startled her, because she jumped. Penelope gave him a decidedly unfriendly look. "It's a combination lock, and a stubborn one at that. I'll probably have more luck with it." She reached in the backseat and got her yellow rain slicker. Then without another word, she pushed open the car door and slammed it behind her.

Brandon watched her in the beam of the headlights as she bent over the lock, rain drizzling down on her. At first, he swallowed his discomfort and his natural inclination to help a woman out.

As the minutes wore on and Penelope seemed to have no success with the lock, the urge to step in became harder to ignore.

When he opened the car door, Penelope lifted her head. "Wait in the car!" she called. "I've almost got it!"

Brandon hesitated for a moment more. Then he yanked the thin poncho he'd bought at the airport over his head and sprinted for the gate. "Here, you're getting soaked."

She looked up at him, eyes blazing. "I said I could get it!"

"What's the big deal, me helping you?"

"Maybe I don't want to take any more help from you. Or maybe I'm insulted that, once again, you think I need rescuing."

"But you do."

"No!" She dropped the lock, which banged against the metal gate, and straightened. The hood of her slicker fell back, leaving her dark hair uncovered. When Brandon tried to put it back on her, she blocked him. "Don't pretend to be nice to me, Brandon, not after giving me the silent treatment the whole car ride over here. Your niceness is…I don't know, Southern manners, a reflex, because you must not trust me or like me. I don't even know why you came along for this trip. I don't know why I wanted to show you the ocean."

"And if you hadn't wanted to, we wouldn't be standing out here in the rain, arguing over who's going to figure out the lock," Brandon told her. "You'd be in your nice warm bed in Bend by now."

"Which is where I should be!" She turned back to work on the lock. "*Arrgh!* Why won't this combination work?"

"Are you sure you've got the—"

"Yes, I'm sure. If you want to be useful, go get the flashlight I keep on my key chain. I think my keys are in the console of the car."

He backtracked to the car through the mud and got the flashlight. Back by her side, he held it over the lock's face and yanked it back when she would have grabbed for it.

"How are you going to hold the light if you've got both hands on the lock?"

"With my teeth, of course."

"Okay, so you've proved that you're superhero tough. Can we just get this lock undone? I'm tired and wet and cranky."

Penelope glared at him. "*I* didn't ask *you* to get out in the rain, so don't expect me to feel sorry for you."

She didn't seem to expect an answer, and he didn't give her one. The rain pelted him on the back, cold and hard through the cheap poncho, as he held the flashlight. Watching her fiddle with the lock was killing him by inches.

He gritted his teeth and held the light and got soaked for his trouble. But then, like the sun parting the clouds after days of rain, Penelope smiled. The lock popped open in her hands. She looked up at him in complete, childlike wonderment.

"I did it! I actually got it!"

Even though he was soaked to the skin, he couldn't help smiling back. "So you did. Now, will you accept a little help to get this gate open? It looks as though it's on the heavy side."

Her smile didn't dim.

Together they pushed the gate back, then dashed for the car.

Now, aided by a dim security light, Brandon could see the house take shape in the darkness as Penelope drove. He squinted for a better look. Two-story clapboard, stark and plain, in a yard that looked maintained but lacked that extra something indicating someone's TLC.

He reached into the backseat for his garment bag and Penelope's overnighter. The thing weighed a ton, but he bit back any complaint. Otherwise, she'd start a whole new argument over who was going to get her bag.

Thankfully the house proved far less of a challenge to get into than the gate had been and Penelope had them in out of the rain before they got any wetter.

She flipped on the lights as she went, revealing a house that was comfortable in a sensible sort of way. Brandon could see gaps in the furniture and on the walls. He hazarded a guess that the best pieces were in someone else's home now.

"Mom said she had the caretaker leave us some bread and milk, basics for breakfast, but if you want anything beyond that, we'll have to forage in town."

Brandon glanced out the window, where the rain was coming down in sheets now. "Nah. That last burger we grabbed at the airport will do me."

"Okay, kitchen's that way, the satellite's cut off, so no TV. Bedrooms are upstairs." Penelope reached for her bag, but Brandon gripped it tighter.

She rolled her eyes. "Fine. I know how heavy that thing was this morning. You want to be my bellboy, that's okay by me." She led the way upstairs.

Halfway up, Brandon spotted a child's crayon drawing on the wainscoting, carefully framed with picture molding. He stopped to examine it: a typical kid-scene of a house and cows and a family, made untypical by the energy of the colors and something he couldn't quite put his finger on. In smaller marker-print at the bottom right, an adult had added, "Penelope, age four."

He called after her, "You did this?"

Penelope halted at the top landing. "What? Oh, that. Yeah. I can't think why Grams never bothered to paint over it."

"You've always been an artist, then."

The observation seemed to catch her unawares. She opened her mouth to speak, but no words came out. Brandon turned back to the picture.

The house in the picture was obviously this house, and the picture was scribbled directly on the wall. Uncle Jake or his mom would have skinned him alive if he'd colored on walls. But someone—her grandmother, maybe—had thought enough of Penelope's talent to cherish it and nourish it.

"It's really good for a four-year-old. I was still doing scribbles then." Brandon realized too late that he was speaking to empty air. Penelope had vanished.

He took the stairs two at a time and headed for the door that was open and the sniffle that was coming from it. Brandon found her sitting on the bed, her face screwed up in an effort not to bawl.

"Hey, what'd I—" He dropped the overnight bag by the door and the garment bag on the bed and knelt in front of her. "Did I say something?"

Penelope shook her head in an abrupt jerk. "I—I'm tired, I think. And Grams isn't getting any younger. Maybe I'm banging my head against a brick wall. But she—she's always believed in me, you know? She was the one who gave me part of the money for the house, said it was an investment. In my career. She's always…"

"But you've never mentioned her. You always said 'the bank.'"

"I did borrow money from the bank. But Grams loaned me money, too, so I didn't have to borrow quite so much at such a high interest rate. Why? What difference does it make?"

Brandon sat back on his heels, trying to suss that out for himself. It did make a difference, somehow.

Penelope chewed on her thumbnail and stared off into the distance. "I hope Mom hasn't told her I lost the commission. She'd be so disappointed that I'm welding farm implements for a living."

He slid a palm against her cheek. Dark ringlets, still damp, brushed against the back of his hand. "If she's the kind of grandmother who framed a four-year-old's scribbles on a wall, she wouldn't. She'd be proud of you for finding a way to make your dream a reality."

Penelope pulled away from him. "Why am I telling you all this? If I fail, you win. You get to pick up the land for a song. Half the time, I suspect all your politeness and good manners are just a salve to ease your guilt. I think that's why you're so kind to me, when you *are*."

"That's not true. I'm kind to you because I want to be." That wasn't strictly true. He hadn't been kind very often, and when he was, it was in spite of *not* wanting to be.

"I could believe that. I could. Except for the way you talk about Grandpa."

He laid a finger against her lips. "Shh. Don't. I've already made that mistake tonight. I'm starting fresh with my promise.

Let's pretend the world ends at Oregon's state line. Just for tonight."

"But we can't, can we?" Penelope started to stand, but he pulled her back down.

"I can try. We have our moments," Brandon said.

"We do. But I can't take it, Brandon. I can't take the guilt that comes from enjoying being around you. Simply being here with you feels like I'm a traitor to—"

"The promise?" he interrupted.

She made a sound in the back of her throat and closed her eyes. "Silly. This is silly."

He ran his hands along her arms, up to her shoulders, along the graceful arc her neck made, and into her curls. Brandon pressed his mouth to her temple, slid his lips down along her cheek. She turned her mouth into his kiss, her lips searching his out. He kissed her and drew back.

Penelope looked up and met his eyes. He opened his mouth to speak, but this time she was the one who silenced him with a finger to his lips. No, there'd be no more talking, no risk of hurt feelings or wounded pride. For them, it seemed, Penelope had decided the world did end at the Oregon state line.

Brandon kissed her finger, opened her palm and pressed a kiss there, too. He saw those hands of hers in a million different memories—building her barn, petting Theo, welding his tractor for him, holding his hand on the airplane.

Without saying a word, he released her hand, slipped her raincoat off her shoulders and tossed it aside.

He kissed away one last tear tracking down her face, followed it as it slid down her cheek to her jaw. She leaned into him as he pressed his lips to hers again.

"You're sure we can forget about Georgia for a while?" Brandon whispered.

She nodded, the very slightest dip of her head.

Penelope drew a fingertip along his face. "The question is," she whispered, not taking her eyes off him, "are you?"

Brandon swallowed the guilt. "I want to." There, that was honest. But did that honesty go far enough? Could he really keep that promise? He captured her fingers in his, opened her hand and pressed a kiss into her palm. He looked up, met her steady questioning gaze. "For you, I'd want to forget every bad thing in the world. And for now, for this trip, I'll give you my very best effort."

She closed her fingers tightly against her palm, as if she were holding onto his kiss. "Okay. I believe you. And I'll try, too. Now beat it, buster. I want to show you the Pacific tomorrow."

The warmth of Penelope's smile speared into him, making him ache to be able to forget Murphy and the farm. He would try. He owed the both of them that much.

CHAPTER TWENTY-FIVE

PENELOPE AWOKE the next morning to find more rain pattering on the window. She propped herself up on one elbow and stared at the raindrops sliding down the pane.

Could the promise she and Brandon had made work? Or was she stupid to think they could bridge the chasm between them? If he cared about her—and when he'd kissed her last night he'd certainly seemed to care— he'd back off hounding Grandpa Murphy into prison, wouldn't he?

You care about him. Does that mean you're ready to sacrifice Grandpa's future so that Brandon can have his dream? You of all people know about dreams.

The clock flashed half-past eight. If she wanted to share the Pacific with Brandon, then she couldn't afford to linger, not if they were going to make their flight to Redmond.

Penelope slid out of bed, jerking back her feet at the coldness of the hardwood floor. She was used to warmer winters already.

She listened intently, but heard no sounds from Brandon in the room next to hers. Penelope opened her palm, where he'd placed his kiss like a gift, a vow, the night before. She laid her palm flat on the wall that separated them—four inches, more or less. Four inches of honor and stubborness and pride, a gap that was maybe a little narrower after their heart-to-heart last night. And today? Today was a brand new start.

With that thought, she banged on the wall. "Hey, sleeping beauty! You awake in there? We'd better get a move on if we're going to make that plane."

Brandon's groan came through the old plaster loud and clear. "Not again. Not another plane. Can't we stay here forever?"

Now that's the answer. If we could stay here, charmed, isolated...

She pushed away the thought. Shower, breakfast, a walk down the beach, and then on to Portland.

"I CAN'T BELIEVE I'm walking in the rain on a beach," Brandon said as they locked the front door. "This is nuts."

"You were the one who wanted to see the Pacific in the fall. What'd you expect? Blue skies? Are you afraid of a little rain? Up here, we're used to the wet stuff." Penelope pointed to the galoshes she'd scored after searching the closets. "And we come prepared."

"I guess up here they come in handy, huh."

Luggage stowed, Penelope turned the car back toward town, and, once she hit Tillamook, made a right toward Cape Meares State Park and the ocean.

The quiet between her and Brandon didn't irritate her like last night's trip had. But she was glad he wasn't talking much. When he talked to her in the way he had this morning, warm and loving, carefully avoiding the subject of Grandpa Murphy, she found herself willing to believe this could last.

On the deserted beach, with the wind and spray and cold rain slicing through her raincoat, Penelope held Brandon's hand and tried not to think of what she'd face back in Georgia. How could she face Grandpa now that she'd gotten close to Brandon? And how could she tell her grandfather that she could never go through with the land sale to the solid-waste company? He needed money for his defense. A federal investigation wasn't going to disappear, as much as she wanted it to.

The incoming tide nibbled at her boots as they headed toward the stark basalt face of Cape Meares. Her choices seemed just as stark.

"Beautiful," Brandon called beside her over the sound of the surf. "Beautiful!"

"Yes, it is!" she called back. Penelope stretched out a hand toward the basalt face. "That's my favorite part of this whole stretch of beach."

He grinned and shook his head. "My favorite part is right here!"

His frank admiration warmed her and re-ignited her guilt. *Traitor. I am a traitor.*

WHAT SEEMED an eternity and another change of planes later, Brandon felt the plane begin its final approach to the Redmond airport and looked out past Penelope to see the unexpectedly stark landscape glow in the afternoon light. Weird how he'd assumed Oregon would be all lush green pines. This looked more like a desert than the home of the Spotted Owl.

He touched Penelope. She stirred from where she'd been nestled against his shoulder, and he flexed his arm gratefully.

She yawned. "Are we there yet?"

"Yeah. I think so, anyway."

Penelope peered out the window. "Yeah, we're closing in on Bend, sweet Bend. Oh, joy."

"You really aren't looking forward to this, are you?"

"Hmm, I don't know. There are worse things," she replied with a laugh. "Root canals. Traffic court."

"What have I got myself into? Are your folks nuts or what?"

"No, they're…not like me. Definitely not like me."

"Your mom seemed nice enough on the phone."

The plane suddenly dropped toward the runway and landed with a few stomach-hurtling bumps. Brandon tried hard to hide how disconcerting it was to him. How could Pe-

nelope sit there so calmly? How had she managed to sleep on the plane?

*Well, you did keep her up talking and kiss-
ing most of the night.*

They hadn't discussed anything about their
future beyond this trip. Brandon was grateful Penelope had seemingly taken to heart
the nothing-beyond-Oregon deal. As long as
they skirted exactly how they were going to
deal with Murphy once they got home, then
Brandon could fool himself into not thinking about it.

It was coming, though. And he couldn't
lie, he was anxious to hear what Marlene
Langston had to tell him about her father.
Maybe some of Murphy's skeletons would
come back to haunt him and show Penelope
exactly who Murphy was.

Off the plane and in the airport, they made
their way past the luggage carousel. Brandon
was shifting his garment bag over his shoulder and dragging Penelope's rolling duffel
behind him when he heard her say, "There
they are."

He looked up to see a tall, slender brunette
waving excitedly.

"Darling!" Marlene Langston greeted her daughter, wrapping her in an effusive embrace.

"Wow, Mom, what a hug! Careful or I'll think you missed me," Penelope told her, returning it.

"Of course I've missed you!" She turned to Brandon and extended a hand. "I'm Marlene Langston, Penelope's mother. And you must be Brandon."

"Yes, ma'am. Thank you for having me."

Marlene craned her head back toward a quiet, silver-haired man waiting behind her. "Peter, did you hear that? Ma'am. He called me *ma'am*. And that accent. Takes me back home."

In person, Brandon could barely detect the slight Southern lilt in Marlene Langston's voice. It was covered by an accent that sounded a lot like Penelope's.

Peter Langston stretched out a hand. "Thank you for taking care of our daughter. I'm afraid she's no good at taking care of herself."

Beside him, Penelope winced. "Dad, you may not like to hear it, but I have managed to survive on my own for several years now. I'm not a complete idiot."

Her father didn't seem convinced in the slightest. His argument was cut short by Marlene steering Penelope toward the exit.

"Peter, I'm sure they're tired—such a long trip from Tillamook—how was the house, dear? Did you get to take Brandon to the beach? Was it raining? The weather here has been terrible, and Jill's mother *insists* on an outdoor wedding for two hundred people. And Jill *insists* on being barefoot. Oh, dear, it's a mess…."

Brandon tried to wrap his mind around a 200-person guest list for a wedding with a barefoot bride. The weddings he'd been dragged to involved hoop skirts and tulle straight out of *Gone With The Wind*. Maybe this one wouldn't be quite so uptight as those.

But his hopes were dashed on the way to the car, as Marlene launched into a long description of the wedding plans. It sounded as complex as any other wedding. Maybe he and Penelope should simply elope.

The errant thought caught him flat-footed.

Had he just been thinking about marrying Penelope?

"Brandon? Did you leave something behind?" Marlene asked.

He realized he'd stood still and let them walk on ahead. "Uh, no."

He didn't have to supply a ready excuse. Marlene walked back, patted him on the arm and said, "Poor fellow is exhausted! Penelope, what have you been doing to him?"

THE DAY OF HER brother's wedding, Penelope woke three hundred fifty dollars poorer than when she'd arrived in Bend. She hadn't been able to endure her mother flipping out her charge card to pay for the J. Crew emerald-green bridesmaid dress and matching shoes. So she'd smiled and dug out her own frail plastic, praying it wouldn't smoke when the clerk zipped it through the card reader.

Penelope took a look at the dress and hung it back up for later. At least it was something they could all agree on. Her mother hadn't been exaggerating when she'd described the battle royal between Trent's future wife and mother-in-law.

In addition to dodging wrangles between

Jill and her mother, Penelope found herself with a to-do list a mile long. Today, her latest and hopefully last mission was to make sure the florist had changed the baby's breath for berries. "More fall, you know? And baby's breath is just so common," Jill's mom had explained. Penelope also had to double-check that the caterer had added pumpkin-colored runners on every table.

Penelope blew out a breath and headed downstairs to grab a bite. Maybe Brandon would want to keep her company.

She found him in the kitchen, nursing a cup of coffee, miraculously alone. Still, she was unsure exactly how to greet him. Would a cheery good morning be what he was after or should she kiss him? Since their arrival in Bend, they'd been plunged back into limbo.

"And I thought you'd been sent on a wedding mission already," Brandon joked.

"On my way out. Last-minute check with the florists and caterer. Mom said she had something to do." As she poured her own cup of coffee, she risked asking, "Why? Have you missed me?"

"Oh, yeah. The minute you appear, they

whisk you away. I can't imagine how insane it would be if it were your own wedding."

For a moment, she let herself have a thirty-second fantasy of a quiet wedding on a beach somewhere, maybe just a couple of witnesses. She jerked back with a start when she realized it was Brandon saying *I do*.

"Trust me, I'm not the two-hundred-guest type," Penelope told him.

"That's a relief."

The coffee in her hand splattered on the counter. He couldn't possibly mean—no, of course not. And why would she think for an instant she wanted him to mean that? Weddings, they completely messed up a girl's mind. Suddenly all those happily-ever-after fantasies came alive. Suddenly even a Mr. Right Now seemed a sure fit to be Mr. Right.

"I was wondering…" Coffee firmly under control, Penelope leaned back against her mother's granite countertop. "Want to go along? Keep me company?"

Brandon grimaced. "Where was it again? Florist and caterer? Can I beg off? That sounds about as exciting as watching paint dry."

"And hanging around here is more exciting? Gee." Penelope took a sip of her coffee to hide her disappointment. "Tells me what a popular gal I am."

"It's—" Brandon screwed up his face as he apparently tried to find words to soften the blow.

She held up a hand. "Don't. It's a guy thing. I can tell."

"Well, your mom had asked me to, uh, help her with something this morning."

Penelope drained her cup and dropped it in the dishwasher. "Poor you. I think I definitely got the better end of the deal."

As she brushed by him, he pulled her down into his lap. "You want me to go, I'll go. After all, even if it is flowers and food, it's got a definite advantage—you."

"It's okay. Really. Don't let my mom work you to death." She gave him a peck on the cheek and headed for her purse and the door.

CHAPTER TWENTY-SIX

BRANDON PEERED out the window, making sure Penelope was backing down the driveway before he sought out Marlene. This whole weekend had been an exercise in frustration for him. On the one hand, he had a devil of a time keeping his mind off Penelope; on the other, he couldn't get Marlene to sit still long enough to give him the dirt on Murphy.

Brandon and Penelope's flight back to Georgia was on Sunday morning. They didn't have much more time here. Marlene had promised last night after the rehearsal dinner, at some sushi place, that she would be ready to talk this morning. He'd been up since five, but for Marlene, weddings apparently took precedent over putting criminals in jail where they belonged.

Be fair. It's her dad. This can't be easy for her.

In the study, Marlene sat down, got up, and

then sat down again, filled with restless energy. Brandon tried to calm her by pretending to relax in a club chair across from her and offering small talk.

But the small talk made her more nervous, not less. "All right, then," Marlene blurted. "You want to know about my father."

"If you're ready to tell me, yes, ma'am."

"My mother says I should let sleeping dogs lie. And I would, ordinarily." Her eyes wide, she clenched and unclenched her fingers. "If he'd never brought Penelope into it, I would have happily let it be. But…my…my daughter."

"Your daughter?" he prompted gently. "What about Penelope?"

"Don't you see? He's using her. He's manipulating her, and because I wouldn't tell her all this when she was young, now she wants to believe her grandfather is a kind old man. She'll close her eyes to everything. That's how Penelope always is, loyal to a fault."

"So why shouldn't she be loyal to Richard Murphy? I mean, I know my reasons. What's yours?"

Brandon let her stew in the indecision that

played over her face. He waited her out, holding his breath.

"My father used to take me along with him when we'd collect the rent," Marlene finally said. "I was maybe eight or so. This was before my parents divorced."

Marlene bounced up from her seat again and walked over to the window. When she spoke, her voice was softer, her Southern accent more pronounced, as though she were channeling who she was in a previous life. "I liked going with Daddy. It didn't matter that the kids I met on those trips were sharecroppers' kids. I liked playing with them. I don't know whether they liked me or whether they played with me because I was the landlord's daughter, but I'd play while Daddy collected the rent."

Brandon tried to be patient.

Marlene went on. "There was one family I liked best. They always played the neatest games, and they had an old tire swing they'd rigged up to look like a horse. I wanted a horse so badly—horse-crazy, Daddy said I was. He wouldn't give me one, told me I wasn't old enough to look after it."

Knew he wouldn't have an animal he couldn't eat. Marlene would have had more luck asking for a pig. Aloud, though, he responded with an, "Uh-huh."

"Their granddaddy lived with them, a black man—the family was black—and I remember one day, in the summer, we went to collect the rent. He was out under a mimosa tree, trying to learn how to read. I felt like such a big girl because I could read it. It was simple, really, but the old man was illiterate, I know that now. So I helped him memorize it. I was so proud." Marlene turned to face Brandon.

He was surprised by the tears in her eyes. Nothing he'd heard should trigger such a powerful response.

Marlene gathered her composure. "I told Daddy on the way home. He acted so proud of me, wanted to know exactly what I'd taught the man. Sweet, oh, he was so sweet. My daddy could charm flies away from honey when he wanted to."

Again, Brandon was confused. What could be so painful about this?

"But later, I heard Mama and Daddy arguing. She wanted him to stay, but he said…all I could gather was that he had to go out. He hit her, that night, when she tried to stop him. I remember crawling in bed beside Mama, holding her as she cried. I was scared, because I'd never seen Mama cry in front of me."

"He abused your mom? Is that why she divorced him?"

But Marlene didn't hear him. "Daddy came into the bedroom when he got in that night. He was…a little drunk, I think now. But he was happy. Satisfied, the way he was after he'd collected all the rents. He told Mama… he told her, I can't remember the words, but something about buying the old man a cocktail. He said, I remember, 'That's the only drink I'll ever buy one of their kind. It was worth losing the house just to show 'em what happens when they get uppity.' He laughed and laughed, like it was the funniest thing. And Mama just cried."

Brandon struggled to put the pieces together. Marlene beat him to the punch, drawing in a strangled breath and wiping away tears. "Mama took me away that night. I didn't understand, not until I was older. The cocktail he'd bought that man was a Molotov cocktail. He'd burnt him out of his house because I'd helped the old man study for the literacy test the man had to take in order to vote."

HALFWAY TO THE CATERER, Penelope realized she'd forgotten the swatch of fabric Jill's mom had decided on for the table runners. She punched in her mom's number, but it went straight to voicemail.

Perfect. Whatever project Mom had Brandon tangled up in had taken them out of the house. Penelope would have to return for the swatch.

Her mother's car was still in the driveway when Penelope pulled back in. Odd. They weren't outside. Had Jill or her mom come by and picked them up?

The swatch was where she'd left it, on the kitchen counter with her notepad of wedding details. But curiosity got the best of her.

Penelope walked through the house until she got to the front hall, off the study. Voices filtered out, her mother's and Brandon's.

"I don't know, I just don't know!" her

mother wept. "I wish I could remember more. My mother refuses to talk about it. Surely someone in the county remembers something."

"I can check. I'll ask Uncle Jake. But, unless someone was killed, arson's statute of limitations ran out years ago. Plus, it was Murphy's house, so it might not even be considered arson. Unless the feds might be interested in tacking on a hate crime or a civil rights violation to Murphy's indictment."

Penelope sucked in a breath, felt suddenly cold. She shoved the study door open.

"What are you doing? Was this the reason you came?"

Her mother put her hands to her mouth. "Oh, Penelope, darling, no. It's not like that at all. He's not interrogating me. I asked him to come. I wanted to—"

"You wanted to what?" Bile rose in her throat. "Make sure Grandpa dies in prison?" She jerked her head toward Brandon, whose face was as green as it had been on the airplane coming here. "You're conspiring with him? You're…I don't know either of you. What's more, I don't think I want to know."

Penelope spun on her heel. Brandon was up now, behind her.

"Wait, Penelope. It's not what you think. Penelope, give me a chance to—"

She barely heard him over her own heaving breaths. She slammed out of the house at a dead run for the car, fumbling for her keys. They slipped from her grasp onto the driveway.

She couldn't scoop them up in time to escape Brandon. He blocked her access to the car. Penelope stared at him, saw him gulp in air from the sprint, and started to push past him.

"Penelope, you've got to hear me out. You owe me that much."

"I don't owe you squat. And if you don't move, I'll lay you on the ground. Don't think I can't."

Brandon stepped aside. "Won't you just listen?"

She snatched open the car door. "So I can what? Hear more lies? Or are you going to try to tell me you and Mom weren't…" Penelope swallowed bile.

"Your grandfather is not who you think he

is or hope he is. And if you'd only listen to your mother…"

Tears scalded the back of her throat. Her mother. Her mother had admitted she'd brought Brandon out here to help plan his attack on an old man who'd die in prison if Penelope didn't do something to stop them.

She threw up both hands, shook her head and got into the car. Penelope put the car in Reverse. Backing out of the driveway, she saw Brandon still standing there, fists clenched by his side, his eyebrows lowered in a glare.

A car horn wailed behind Penelope and she stomped on the brake to avoid backing into the passing car. Brandon took a step toward her, but a quick glance in the mirror told her the road was clear. She backed out, not caring which direction she took. Anywhere but here.

At the end of her parents' street, she stopped the car and gasped for breath. Tears streamed down her face.

I have to do something.

Penelope fumbled through her purse for her cell phone. With fingers that trembled so much she had to redial, she punched in the digits.

"Grandpa? Grandpa, you were right. I—I…" She sobbed, leaning against the steering wheel. "I can't trust Brandon. He…" She couldn't bear to tell him about his own daughter turning traitor. "Whatever you need me to do, I'm ready to do it. Okay?"

On the other end of the line, she heard him breathe out a long sigh. "Well, now, Penny-girl," he said in the gentlest of tones. "Well, now. I knew I could count on you."

CHAPTER TWENTY-SEVEN

BRANDON RESTED his hands on the fence and stared at Penelope's little house. She'd been avoiding him for days. He no longer saw her on her back porch in the mornings. She was conspicuously absent, though her car was in the driveway, whenever he'd come by to try to talk some sense into her.

The flight home had been quiet and tense, and this time not due to Brandon's dislike of flying.

After Penelope had caught him and Marlene talking about Murphy, the weekend was a bust. He'd tried everything, but Penelope had refused to listen to anything either he or Marlene said. Whenever she would meet his eyes, her huge dark ones overflowed with hurt.

Why does it have to come down to this choice of Murphy over me? Over common human decency? He's a crook. He's not worth the consideration Penelope has in her little finger.

Brandon started to turn. As he did, an engine's thrum filled the air and a small dark helicopter circled overhead. The helicopter seemed to be searching out a landing spot and it found it, all right, in the middle of his just-planted, barely sprouted winter wheat.

With a hand on a metal post and a foot in the wire, Brandon jumped the fence and started toward the idiots. Couldn't they see they'd landed in a cultivated field?

The blades slowed as Brandon approached the helicopter. A slick *GQ* type and a rotund little man with maybe three strands of blond hair across his pink scalp ducked under the blades and jogged over to meet Brandon.

"Hi, there," the *GQ* type shouted over the dying noise of the helicopter's blades. "I'm Todd Jeffers with Mid-Florida Environmental Solutions! Are you here to meet us?"

If the introduction was supposed to clue Brandon in, it didn't. "You're in my field!" he snapped. "You just landed that helicopter in my field!"

From somewhere behind him, Murphy said, "I told them they could."

Brandon had that oh-so-familiar stomach-churning reaction to Murphy's smug voice. He turned to see Penelope and Murphy closing the gap between them.

"Hi, there!" Penelope held out a hand to the strangers. "I'm Penelope Langston. You're Rudy Richardson and Todd Jeffers?"

The rotund man wiped a forearm across his perspiring face and then accepted Penelope's hand. "Yes, I'm Rudy!" He turned to Brandon. "Sorry if we messed anything up. My pilot there—" he jabbed a thumb in the direction of the helicopter "—said it was as good a place to land as any."

Brandon started to speak but found he couldn't. He looked at Penelope, who was looking at where the helicopter had landed.

She said in a halting voice, "I…I'd said you could land close to the pond. That's Brandon's winter wheat."

"And *I* said they could land anywhere they wanted," Murphy repeated, jabbing his thumb against his chest. "After all, when we sell this part of the land, they can do whatever they please."

"Sell? Penelope? You're selling? But you…I wanted…" Brandon broke off as he saw the softness in Penelope's expression turn hard and cold.

"You made it perfectly clear what you wanted in Oregon. Guys? I think we'll have more privacy in the house."

PENELOPE LED the way past her barn and into the kitchen. Chairs scraped on the old linoleum as everyone took a seat. For a moment, she was swept away in memories of how Brandon and she had shared more than one meal at this table. Through the window, she let her gaze follow Brandon's departing, ever-smaller figure across the field and then stared at the helicopter. It looked like a huge black widow in the middle of Brandon's winter wheat.

Why, after she knew what he wanted to do to her grandfather, after she'd caught him red-handed, couldn't this be easier? Why did she still feel…remorse? Love? Could she love him? Could she love a man she'd had all wrong?

I shouldn't have gotten close to him.

She dragged her attention back to the conversation unfolding. This Grandpa Murphy sounded completely different from the one she'd come to know. He was slick and professional, with facts and figures at his fingertips.

When Rudy wanted to know about workforce potential, Grandpa tossed off high school graduation rates with the casual ease of a chamber of commerce director. When Todd wanted to know the depth and the flood stage of the creek, Grandpa replied without hesitation. When Rudy asked about the abandoned rail spur on the property, Grandpa referred him to the railroad's owner and recapped a conversation he'd had with the man.

Penelope's stomach churned. She didn't know this Grandpa Murphy at all.

"You have no idea what a pleasure it is talking with you. This parcel seems perfect, based on what you've said. Of course…" Rudy narrowed his eyes. "I've thought that before. That's why we keep coming back to you on this land. This makes the fourth 'perfect' piece of land I've looked at for this project. Something always goes south at the last minute, and I can tell you, I'm real tired of shucking out option money for property we don't acquire."

"So if your project is so great for the community, why aren't more towns vying for it?" Penelope couldn't help asking.

Grandpa shot her a warning look.

"Good question," Rudy answered, sitting back in his chair. "Tell me and we'll both know. All you have to do is say the words 'solid-waste facility' and people start screaming. They won't even listen. They picket their county commissions. They picket their land-use boards. They scream about how we're trucking in garbage."

"But they have a point," Penelope said, ignoring Grandpa's intake of breath.

"People don't understand. You use this stuff, you put it in the trash, somebody's gotta do something with it. At least I'm sorting it and recycling what I can. It's all done by computer, using robotic equipment. It goes in as mountains of garbage, and it either comes out as recyclable plastic or paper or very clean smoke and steam."

Todd leaned across the table and tapped

the copy of the plat they'd been studying. "That's why our company is willing to pay you at least twice what the market value is for this land. Because, even though Brazelton County has no zoning or land-use ordinances in its incorporated areas, Rudy knows you're going to have to deal with a lot of grief. And because, frankly, his investors are getting nervous. If Rudy doesn't get the ground-breaking done on this within the next year, well…"

"Now, Todd, let's not make it sound so dire. Yeah, my money guys want me to expand, and they're willing to pony up the dollars to do that. They're not going to wait forever, that's true enough."

Penelope examined the facility's blueprints. It looked full to the brim of modern technology and robotics. "But how many actual jobs would this bring to the community?"

Todd and Rudy exchanged a brief look. "Well, you know, nobody actually wants to handle garbage. So we use a lot of equipment."

"How many jobs?" she insisted.

"Maybe twenty-five, fifty, to start."

"And then?"

"Well, it depends. On company profits and feasibility."

Rudy must have seen she wasn't pleased with Todd's answer. "Of course we'll add more jobs. But this is a poor area of the state, Ms. Langston. And any jobs are better than no jobs. Plus, these will be high-paying jobs."

They answered her other questions with something Penelope could only call slick. Grandpa seemed to buy their pat answers.

She willed him to see through it, to see these two as she saw them. Couldn't he see the way they hesitated, a fraction, before answering? How they put their fingers to their mouths as they replied to one of her tougher questions?

Maybe he does notice, but he's not saying anything.

Grandpa Murphy remained upbeat as the four of them rode out to the abandoned rail spur at the far end of Penelope's land.

Rudy stomped around, shaded his eyes and nodded in satisfaction. "Creek's that way?" he asked.

"Yes," Penelope said. "And that's an unpaved county road that divides the property."

"You'd have to talk to the county commission," Grandpa said, "but since this road has no houses on it now, I'd say that a quitclaim was a definite probability."

"Perfect," Rudy said. "I like it. This looks perfect."

"Now, to show you we're seriously interested in this parcel, we're willing to put up a quarter of the purchase price as an option payment," Todd said. The way he fixed his eyes on Penelope in a hard, assessing stare reminded her of a rattler just before it strikes. "Of course, for that much in-earnest money, we'll need a fairly in-depth options contract."

"Of course," Grandpa replied for her. "You folks want to be sure you've got a deal." Penelope wanted to shake him, to yell at him until he came out of whatever kind of spell this was.

Grandpa gave her a meaningful glance and jerked his head. He obviously expected her to say something at this point.

Say what? "Where's the dotted line?"

Penelope cleared her throat. "You can talk

big fat percentages all you want, but until you make me a firm offer, I can't possibly entertain tying up the land."

Todd and Rudy looked at each other. Rudy nodded almost imperceptibly.

"Well…" Todd covered his mouth again and cleared his throat. "Providing all this checks out, of course, we're prepared to offer you ten grand."

Penelope laughed. The constriction around her lungs eased at the lowball price they'd given her. She could turn this offer down immediately. "Ten thousand? You have got to be out of your mind!"

Todd looked to Rudy and when Rudy nodded again, Todd said, "Okay, we'll go to fifteen grand an acre, but that's it."

"Fifteen thousand an acre?" she choked out. "For twenty-five acres?"

"Anything else, and we have to get approval from our full board of directors," Rudy told her. "But give us a firm option today, and we can write you a check for a quarter of that."

Three hundred seventy-five thousand dollars? For farmland she paid two thousand an acre for? What kind of operation were they putting here?

Penelope's senses went on full alert. She glanced from Rudy to Todd to Grandpa Murphy, all eagerness for her to say yes.

She couldn't endure it. She wheeled slowly around. Her eyes followed the lay of the land as she made her turn. Could she do this? Could she sell this land out from under Brandon and let it be scarred by garbage?

She spotted Brandon at the fence. He was watching them, she realized. This time, he didn't stand so straight. This time, even from this distance, she could see how his whole body drooped in defeat.

In one fell swoop, she could rescue her grandfather, give him all the resources he needed for his legal defense, and she could wound Brandon where it hurt the most.

Say no.

Grandpa Murphy jostled her elbow. In her ear, he muttered, "Penny-girl, they're waiting! This money will help me pay my lawyers, keep me out of prison. I gotta have it. Tell 'em yes."

She tore her gaze from Brandon. "Grandpa,"

she said, patting him on the chest. "We have to be sure. Besides…" How to buy time? "If they'll pay fifteen, who's to say they won't pay twenty?"

Her grandfather's eyes lit up. "Now you're thinking like a businesswoman. You're right, don't look too eager."

Penelope addressed Rudy and Todd. "I think to short-circuit all that community protest you talked about, perhaps you should meet with the county commissioners, maybe even have a public hearing."

They didn't look happy. "Well, we're not required—there's no zoning ordinance," Todd said.

"My grandfather's assured me of that. But I'd like to do this as transparently as possible. So? What's your answer?"

CHAPTER TWENTY-EIGHT

BRANDON SAT on the end of Ryan MacIntosh's dock, a handful of pebbles in his hand. Ryan and Sean Courtland leaned up against the dock's railing.

When he tossed the pebbles, one by one, instead of skipping across the surface of the dark water, most of them sank.

"So these waste dump people, they're on the up-and-up?" Brandon asked. He'd called Sean from the field that day, gave him the name of Mid-Florida Environmental and asked him to find out what he could. It had only taken a couple of days for Sean to get the information, but by then, it was common knowledge Penelope was selling out.

Sean hesitated. "Well, no mob connections that I can find out. That's the first thing I thought of when you said waste disposal. They've been in business for about ten years, very profitable, but they're running out of dumping room. They specialize in medical waste, biohazards, stuff like that."

"I hear it's all automatic," Ryan said. "They're hiring maybe fifty people, and that would cover all three shifts."

"They believe in technology, robotics. In Florida at their main facility, as technology improved, they gradually cut their work-force. They had about two hundred when they opened, but now they're dealing with twice the volume and they've got half the employees. So I wouldn't be surprised in a couple of years if that employee count was slashed."

"So why here?" Brandon asked. "How'd Penelope find them so quick?"

Sean dropped down beside him. "My sources tell me they've been looking for land without zoning ordinances, but with water and access to a railroad. That's been hard to find. They've been turned down in three counties in South Georgia so far. This land fits the bill."

"But that begs the question, how'd they find this place?"

"Maybe Murphy's been working with

them, and the auction interrupted his deal," Ryan speculated.

"So Penelope knew? All this time?" Brandon slung the entire handful of pebbles into the pond. "And she never told me?"

"Do you think she knew?" Sean asked.

Brandon thought back to the argument she and Murphy had before they left for Oregon. "We'll discuss this when we get back," Penelope had said.

He sprang up from the dock so fast his foot connected with Sean's leg, eliciting a "Hey, watch it" from Sean. "Sorry, man. I think she did know. Something happened…" He choked out the events of that morning, ending with, "I thought she was worked up because she wanted him out of her house. But maybe she was afraid he'd say something to me about this sale. She had me played. I cannot *believe* I fell for her wide-eyed Miss Innocent look. I built her a *barn!*"

"So what are you going to do?" Ryan asked.

"What can I do? There's no zoning ordinance in this county. I tried to tell people we needed land-use regulations, but no, no, they wouldn't believe me. I guess they'll believe me now when they're downwind from a garbage dump." Brandon paced the dock, his hold on his temper slipping with every Penelope moment he recalled.

"There's that meeting you told us about," Sean reminded him.

"Fat lot of good that will do me. The county can't do squat without some sort of zoning, and any zoning they pass now would be after the fact."

"Yeah, but Brandon, you're forgetting something," Ryan said. "They got run out of three counties already. Why was that?"

Brandon stopped. "Yeah. That's right. Sean, how did the counties fight back?"

"They changed the owners' minds. Protests, petitions, signs, mass public awareness meetings. You name it, they did it. The owners backed out, because they knew they wouldn't be welcome there if they did sell."

Could Penelope be so heartless that she would go through with this if she heard how it affected the community? He had seen her crying on that bed in her grandmother's house, seen the softness in her expression after he'd kissed her. Her hand in his on the beach....

It can't all have been an act.

He berated himself for the stubborn hope that wouldn't be extinguished.

Ryan propped a foot on the railing. "Murphy's been bragging all over town that this money will buy him enough legal horsepower to shake off the federal indictment."

"Good luck to him then." Sean grinned. "The way I hear it, the deputy U.S. attorney's just about ready to present to the grand jury, and you know what that means. He thinks he's got that airtight case he's been looking for. So Murphy might as well take a match and burn that money up."

"Yeah, but." Brandon couldn't take it anymore. He walked back up the dock, toward the grass and his truck, his footfalls echoing in the quiet of the early evening.

"Yeah, but what?" Ryan called after him.

"The land will still be gone. And this time...forever."

WHEN PENELOPE HAD been four, Trent had talked her into going down the big, curvy slide. She'd thought she was ready—until she'd managed the climb up the fourteen steps to the top of the slide.

Trent had been behind her, huffing with the imperious impatience of a nine-year-old. "C'mon, Penny! Mom's gonna tell us we gotta go! So move, will ya?"

When she'd whimpered and wanted to go back, Trent had stuck his tongue out at her and sneered. "Baby! You're a widdle-bitty baby!"

So she'd done it. She'd turned around, settled on the top of the slide and let gravity take over. A fraction of a second after she'd let go, before the first hairpin turn, all her doubts supersized into gigantic screaming monsters. She wanted to stop. She wanted off.

Instead, she'd been sucked along on three more curves before she'd been able to set her shaky knees on solid ground.

All these years later, Penelope was beginning to get the same feeling she'd had on that slide.

The Dyno-Trash-Duo as she'd taken to calling them to herself, had scheduled the meeting as she requested. It had a downside she hadn't calculated. Now everybody in the county knew the company's intentions and blamed her.

She pulled into the crammed parking lot of the county board office. Conversations hushed as Penelope pushed through the crowd gathering on the lawn and spilling out of the commission office onto the old-fashioned front porch. From the rubbernecking, it was clear Penelope had been the central topic of discussion.

Inside the boardroom, Penelope nodded at Rudy, seated in the front row of stackable chairs, and at Todd, who was busy setting up a PowerPoint program. Grandpa Murphy was standing beside Rudy and waved her over.

"Whew," Penelope told her grandfather. "Those guys out there sounded like they were after my blood."

He laughed. "If they'd had a chance to switch places with you, darlin', they would. In a heartbeat. Let 'em complain. It'll give them something to do while you and I are on our way to the bank."

A few minutes later, the chairman of the county commission took his seat. He brought the meeting to order with a stern warning about the consequences of disruption. "We'll hear from folks in a civilized, courteous manner—from all sides—and then we'll give you the county's legal position."

First up was Rudy, his pink scalp gleaming through his comb-over. With the help of Todd's PowerPoint presentation, he made a pitch to the board about the solid-waste facility, how it would bring jobs and tax revenue to the county, how technologically advanced it was.

"We're not asking for any county tax abatement. We're not asking for the county to pony up any funds, just the quitclaim deed to the county road that bisects the land we intend to buy," Rudy finished up.

"Hogwash," somebody from the back piped up, and the room erupted into bedlam.

CHAPTER TWENTY-NINE

THE CHAIRMAN RAPPED his gavel for order. "I have here a list of people who have actually taken the trouble to get on the agenda. Now, I'm not going to be here all night, and the board's got some other matters to tend to, so y'all keep this short and remember to share the time."

One by one, they came. Penelope recognized more than a few as people who'd helped build her barn. She felt her stomach turn over as she heard their disappointment and anger. A few of them even mentioned the barn raising, and how they'd been affronted by her willingness to betray their hospitality.

"Least she could have done," one farmer said, "was tell me about it herself. Instead, I find out about it through the grapevine." He sat down, shaking his head.

When Penelope glanced behind her at the

crowd standing, she saw Uncle Jake leaning against the doorjamb, near Brandon.

Would either of the two of them speak up against the land deal?

"Well, now," the chairman said, "we've got one more person on the list. Brandon, what do you have to say about all this?"

The crowd's muttering ceased. Brandon rose from his folding chair and strode up to the podium set before the commissioners. Instead of addressing them, he turned and faced the crowd.

"I heard all of what you said tonight." He nodded in the direction of a couple of people who'd spoken already. "And I couldn't agree more. I don't have a lot to add. The land they're buying is the best land in the county, at least I think so. Most of the farmers here would agree. It's wrong to see it used for a facility that will only hurt the community." His voice cracked with emotion at these last words. "It's made even worse because we trusted Penelope. We trusted her and reached out to her—in spite of who her grandfather was."

Beside her, Grandpa Murphy stiffened and

started to rise. Penelope saw Rudy put a restraining hand on him. Grandpa didn't look happy, but he made no further move to get up.

"We all know what this money is going for," Brandon continued. "It's not to help her have a better living here—no one could blame someone for that. No, this money will go to Richard Murphy's attorneys. Now you decide. Is that something we should support?"

The grumbling and murmuring grew louder, and angry hisses came from all corners of the room.

Brandon waited, silent for a long moment, while the tension built. "If it's not, then the only person who can control this, the one person who can make this all go away, is sitting right over there." He pointed to Penelope. "It's her land, at least, that's what the title says. So you tell her if you have a problem with it. *You* tell her. As for me, she knows how I feel." Brandon's mouth twisted. "She knows, and she's doing this anyway. She's not one of us. This deal tells me she'll never be."

Under his accusing stare, Penelope dropped her gaze to her hands in her lap.

How can I feel so guilty about this? If only he'd back off, give Grandpa—and me—some breathing room.

When she looked back up, he was already moving to the door.

The chairman of the commissioners leaned forward and spoke into his mike. "I think it's clear here how the public feels about this. But, folks, according to our lawyer, there's not one whit that can be done about it. We got no zoning ordinance, no land-use ordinance—something the county residents voted down two to one just a few years ago. It's Penelope Langston's land, and she's got the unbridled right to do whatever she wants to with it."

Penelope barely noticed the grumbles of discontent in the audience. She couldn't think of anything except what Brandon had said.

The chairman rapped his gavel again. "Now, as we can take no action on this, we're going to move on to the next portion of the meeting."

Grandpa Murphy startled her when he leaned down and whispered in her ear, "Let's get out of here, nothing more they can do to us. We've sat through their public flogging. Now we can do what we please."

He followed in Brandon's wake. For a moment, Penelope simply sat there, too numb to move. Then she saw Rudy follow Grandpa, and Todd hurrying to pack up his equipment. She crossed over to the table and began helping him. Her fingers fumbled with electrical cords and cables, and she dropped one of them. Todd retrieved it.

"Hey, don't let them get to you," he whispered. "That's nothing compared to what we've seen before."

Right. Nothing. A man she loved—her heart squeezed at this realization... How could this have happened? How could she have fallen in love with someone who wished so much ill on her family?

Outside, Brandon was nowhere to be seen. Rudy and Grandpa were talking near Rudy's rental car.

Todd let the door close by itself as he came out to join her. "Glad that's over," he said as he shifted his laptop case and the projector in his hands. "I wasn't kidding when I said it was nothing compared to other communities. We should have taken Mr. Murphy up on his offer when he first came to us three years ago."

"You mean two." Penelope pulled her jacket tighter around herself. "He's only had the land for two."

"Oh, no. It was three. I remember. We'd been run out of one county, and he'd heard about it. Came to us and said he had his eye on a piece of land he could pick up for a song and wanted to know if we were interested. At the time, I hate to admit it, but I thought he was shooting off at the mouth. I mean, the property might have been perfect, but it wasn't even his and the owner at the time told us he wasn't interested in selling at any price. Guy hung up on us as quickly as if we'd been aluminum siding salesmen. Wouldn't even listen or take down our contact information. But your grandfather pulled it off, just like he said he would, and now we'll all be sitting pretty."

The blood turned to ice in Penelope's veins. The late evening swirled around her. She grabbed for anything to keep her knees from buckling.

"Are you okay?" Todd's voice seemed to come from a distant place.

She shook her head. She'd never be okay, never, ever. Her grandfather had lied to her—Brandon had been right. Grandpa Murphy had wanted Uncle Jake's land three years ago, for this. He'd played her. All along, he'd played her.

What have I done?

The bile rose in her throat. She had lost Brandon, and for what?

She dashed back inside and made the turn into the ladies' room. Falling down in front of the lone toilet, the cold tile floor biting into her knees, Penelope retched.

CHAPTER THIRTY

WHEN SHE CAME out of the bathroom, Grandpa Murphy was waiting for her in the anteroom of the commission offices. "Penny-girl, you sick? Todd said—"

"I'm not selling."

"What?" At first, he went slack jawed with disbelief. Then he smiled and reached out to touch her. "Don't let 'em get you down, Penny-girl. Life's not a popularity test."

"I mean it. I'm not selling."

"Because a bunch of complainers and whiners flapped their jaws?"

"Because I know how long you've been working on this deal. Brandon was right, wasn't he? You did steal that land from Uncle Jake. You stole it so you could sell it to them." She jerked her head out the door where Rudy and Todd waited, concern on their faces.

"Who cares how I got it? It's mine."

"No. That's where you're wrong, Grandpa.

The land is mine. And I do care how you got it. I can't sleep at night knowing you'll profit from whatever deal you made to get this land."

He grabbed her by the arm, shook her. "Now you listen here, girl. I need that money. Three years ago, it was just a nice little cherry on the top, but now I need it! And you're gonna get it for me. That money's mine, and I worked hard to get it."

Her reflexes kicked in before she could even think. With a sharp jab to the instep of his foot and an elbow in his soft belly, she was free. He staggered backward. "Penny-girl, you're acting like a stranger."

"You didn't work hard to get that land." Her stomach churned, but there was nothing else to come up. "You stole it. To me, you are a stranger."

UNCLE JAKE LOOKED up from the piece of paper in his hand. "Penelope, are you sure you want to do this?"

"Yes. I can't keep this land a minute lon-ger."

"But…you're giving it to me, well, selling

it for a dollar. And now you've got that nice little house on it…"

She could almost weep at the thought of leaving the first home of her own, but she shook her head. She'd known it was useless to stay when Brandon wouldn't even listen to her after the meeting. "No, you're not going to change my mind. I'll pack everything, put it in storage, something."

"Darlin', you're upset. Wait at least until morning. I would be no gentleman to sign this here paper. It would be taking advantage of you in the worst way."

She pushed the chair back from the old man's table. "I'm leaving. I can't stay here. I can't—not after—" Penelope swallowed, her throat tight. "I'm flying back to Oregon. To-night. And I won't be back. So consider the land yours. It is yours. It was never mine, and I'll figure out some way to pay off the loan."

"Oregon?" Uncle Jake shook his head. "You got to go tonight?"

"Yes. I've got—I've got a lot of patching up to do with my mother. At least, I hope she's not like Brandon and she'll still forgive me."

Uncle Jake traced a spot on the papers with

a gnarled finger. "Now, girl, you listen to me. That Brandon is stubborn. Of course he is, 'cause he is a Wilkes. But let me tell you, all he's doing is kicking the tires of a broke tractor. You walk off now, well, you know what happens to tractors that get left."

She drew in a shaky breath. "But Uncle Jake, I'm the one who broke that tractor for him. And I don't blame him. Because after all is said and done, I don't deserve a chance."

A MONTH LATER, Brandon knelt down, inspecting the piping that irrigated his strawberries. The cool earth yielded to the weight of his knee. His uncle's soil. Once again, this land was back where it belonged.

He hadn't understood what exactly had been the breaking point for Penelope. At first, he was just glad she was gone and she'd refused to sell to the waste-dump people.

The land is safe. That's what you wanted. Right? And you can be content with that.

But Brandon couldn't help but look at the dark, silent house. The doors on the barn were shut, but he'd seen the moving truck come in after Penelope had left. They'd cleaned out the barn. It was cold and empty.

Like your heart.

Uncle Jake walked stiff legged through the field, no fence blocking his way. First thing Brandon had done was finish tearing it down.

"You're looking in the wrong place," Uncle Jake shouted.

"For what?"

"For Penelope. You won't find her here."

Brandon froze. "Who says I'm looking for her?"

Uncle Jake hitched up his overalls. "Maybe you're not. Maybe all this mooning around you been doing is what every fellow does when he finally gets what he wants."

"I'm not—" Brandon rubbed a hand over his face. Who was he fooling, anyway? Not Uncle Jake.

Geraldine had followed her master and was now trotting through Brandon's strawberries, delicately nosing around to see if there was any ripe fruit.

"Now, Geraldine!" Uncle Jake scolded. "Out of them strawberries, and don't you step on a single plant."

The hog high-stepped it over the rows.

Uncle Jake, apparently satisfied with his pet pig, turned back to Brandon.

"Now, all this mooning around you say you're *not* doing, well, it's what a fellow does when he gets what he *thinks* he wants." The old man put his fingers to his lips and gave a shrill whistle. "C'mon, Geraldine. No more fun and games for you, old girl. You get out of that pen one more time today, and it's pork chops for you, no matter how much you bat your eyes at me. Pork chops, I say, and this time I mean it."

PENELOPE RUBBED her eyes and erased an errant line off her sketch paper so hard she tore a hole. She had to get this right, and nothing was working.

Crumpling up the paper, she tossed it on the overflowing heap in the wastebasket. Theo lifted his head and looked at her in disgust, his slumber interrupted.

How can you create anything with a broken heart?

But this chance—a much smaller project than *Love at Infinity*—wouldn't wait around forever, no matter if forever was what it felt like it would take to heal. The company wanted her final sketch and model by the end of the week.

She looked around her grandmother's living room. It would do for now. Even if it was a drafty old place and she couldn't hear the frogs sing at night like she had in Georgia.

And you don't have Brandon.

A million times she'd picked up the phone to call him, then put it down. After all, in all these weeks, he hadn't called her. If he hung up on her, she didn't think she could take it. What was she after anyway? Forgiveness?

Your heart. You're after your heart. You left it in Georgia.

Over the drum of rain on the windows, Penelope heard loud knocking. She frowned. Who—her mom? That's who it had to be. Her mom should have never driven over the mountains in this weather.

But when Penelope opened the door, Brandon, soaking wet, stood waiting to be let in.

BRANDON STOOD just inside the door, his clothes stuck to him, his heart in his throat.

How could he get the words out when he didn't know what to say?

"How—how did you get here?" Penelope asked as she pushed the door shut.

"A plane. And a pill the doctor said would take the edge off my fear of flying laid me flat. That's why I wasn't here yesterday. I thought I should stay overnight in Portland and, uh, sleep off my anesthesia at a hotel."

"You flew? By yourself? But you hate flying."

"I needed—"

"If it's about the land," she started, "if there's anything wrong with the title or— I'll fix it."

"Yeah. There's something wrong with the land," Brandon managed to get out.

"What? I thought I'd taken care of everything." She frowned and turned. "C'mon in. Forgive the place, I've been working on a project." She stopped so suddenly that Brandon nearly cannoned into her. "Can I take your coat?"

"Uh, yeah." Why couldn't he just say it? Why was he wasting all this time with small talk?

She slid the coat from his shoulders, her hands lightly skimming over his damp shirt. "I'll hang this in the bathroom."

"No, Penelope, wait. I wanted to tell you what was wrong with the land."

She stopped again, coat dripping in her hand. "I'll fix it. I mean it. Whatever it is. It's Uncle Jake's land, and I was wrong not to believe you. I—I'm sorry. I should have… should have known."

"That you had a criminal for a grandfather? Nobody wants to believe that. And even crooks have granddaughters."

Penelope looked away. "Mom told me, finally. About the arson. I wish she'd told me years ago." She twisted the collar of the coat in her hands and more water oozed out. "This coat, it's dripping. Let me—"

Brandon took it from her and slung it on the nearby table. "Forget the coat," he told her, but the words came out hoarse. "Listen. Please, listen. I thought everything was right again when you left and Uncle Jake had the land—"

"Just tell me what's wrong!" Her voice broke.

"You. You're what's wrong. You're not there." For a panicked moment, Brandon thought he might actually cry. He sucked it up, put a lid on his emotions.

"Me? But you didn't want me."

"I didn't know what I wanted. But I do now. Penelope, I flew on a plane to get here. That ought to tell you something." He gulped, his throat dry. "The question isn't what I want. It's what you want. We've been concentrating on what I want—or what I thought I wanted—for way too long."

Brandon's heart banged against his ribs as he waited for her answer. As she started to speak, his cell phone buzzed.

He yanked it out of his pocket to turn it off, but saw the sheriff's department on the caller ID. "Hello?"

"Brandon? That you? Are you really in Oregon? 'Cause it sounds like you're right here in Brazelton County."

"Prentice. What are you doing tying up the department's line?"

"Sheriff let me. Said I could. Have you asked Penelope to marry you? Did she say yes? Is she coming back? 'Cause I wanna see that alien man and woman she's fixing up."

"Prentice, I don't know if she's going to marry me, because I haven't asked her yet." Brandon realized what he'd said. He took in Penelope's face, her eyes tearing up, her smile as radiant as the day he first met her. "But you know what, Prentice? I'm gonna hang up and ask her right now."

"Call me back! And I'll tell everybody! Brandon and Penelope sitting in a tree, k-i-s-s-i-n-g—"

Brandon closed the phone and tossed it to join his coat. "Uh, I really made a hash of that, didn't I?"

"I can't think of a more beautiful proposal," Penelope whispered.

"So…what you want is…what?"

"Home. I want to go home. With you. And hold your hand on the plane. And see my house—your house—"

"Our house."

She nodded. "Our house. Can we go home?"

"I was sure hoping you'd say so. I don't have a ring yet, but will a slightly soggy, nonrefundable one-way ticket to Savannah do for now?"

"Perfectly." A frown marred her forehead. "But we've got to see about Theo—"

"Of course. I checked on that. It's all taken care of."

Penelope reached up and kissed him. "Did you?"

"Cat's part of the package. Like Uncle Jake's Geraldine."

"I've missed Geraldine. And Uncle Jake. And Prentice." She laid her head on his chest, not complaining about how damp his shirt was.

"You know Prentice will insist on being the best man."

"As long as you're the groom, and I'm the bride. That's what I want."

Brandon tipped up Penelope's face to kiss her again. "And I've got what I want right here."

* * * * *